Sherlock Holmes
and
The Sandringham House Mystery

By the same author

Sherlock Holmes and the Egyptian Hall Adventure
Sherlock Holmes and the Eminent Thespian
Sherlock Holmes and the Brighton Pavilion Mystery
Sherlock Holmes and the Houdini Birthright
Sherlock Holmes and the Man Who Lost Himself
Sherlock Holmes and the Greyfriars School Mystery
Sherlock Holmes and the Yule-tide Mystery
Sherlock Holmes and the Theatre of Death
Sherlock Holmes and The Baker Street Dozen
Sherlock Holmes and the Circus of Fear

Sherlock Holmes
and
The Sandringham House Mystery

Val Andrews

**BREESE
BOOKS
LONDON**

First published in 1998 by
Breese Books Ltd
164 Kensington Park Road, London W11 2ER, England

© Breese Books Ltd, 1998

ISBN: 0-947533-53-2

Typeset in 11½/14pt Caslon by
Ann Buchan (Typesetters), Middlesex
Printed and bound in Great Britain by
Itchen Printers Ltd, Southampton

CHAPTER ONE

The Agitated Illusionist

'By Jove, Holmes, it's a real pea-souper!'

The November of 1902 was living up to that season's reputation and I could scarce see the other side of Baker Street from the front window of number 221B. But my friend Mr Sherlock Holmes seemed rather uninterested in my remarks concerning the weather; however, he lowered his newspaper and spoke to me for the first time in almost an hour.

'Watson, the fog interests me only in that it could confuse my expected caller in finding his way here. He is, you see, not native to the shores, although I believe he is well known in theatrical circles.'

'Don't tell me that George Robey has lost the latest violin that he has been fashioning in his dressing-room, or that Marie Lloyd has lost her famous parasol?' I could not resist airing what little knowledge I had upon current theatre topics.

'Interesting, Watson, that your mind leapt straight to music-hall celebrities rather than to the actors of the legitimate stage.'

'I can only suggest that my mind did so because music-hall performers seem more likely to be in need of your services on account of their somewhat more bohemian style of living. I can hardly imagine Sir Henry Irving requiring the services of a consulting detective.'

Holmes smiled indulgently and expressed his interest in my theory, then he pointed to a silk hat which hung from the stand in the corner. 'The gentleman concerned left his hat behind when he called during our absence. He did not leave a card but told Mrs Hudson that he would return today at twelve of the clock to consult me upon a matter of some delicacy. It is now fifteen minutes short of midday, so let us pass that quarter of an hour in deducing what we can of our expected visitor. I did not ask the good lady much concerning him, not wishing to lose the pleasure of such an exercise. Come, Watson; you are familiar enough with my methods. Pray tell me what you can concerning the owner of the hat.'

I took the silk hat from the stand and examined it carefully in what light I could find. There was little enough from the window so I was obliged to light the gas and turn it up until it hissed. How my friend had been able to read the newspaper without the aid of spectacles in such a poor light was beyond me; but I had always felt that he had the eyes of an eagle. The hat was of good quality and I was soon able to make a few simple observations.

'Well, Holmes, I find that the hat belongs to a prosperous American of quite advanced years. I would expect him to be immaculate in his appearance; probably tall and slim.'

Holmes took the hat from my hands and was critical in his tones. 'Interesting deductions, Watson, but not entirely accurate.'

'You mean I have missed something of moment?'

'Misinterpreted the information that you saw before you, Watson. You are basing your deduction concerning his nationality upon the maker's name inside the hat: Dudkin and Son, Hatters, Brooklyn. But I have a hat which I sometimes wear which bears a maker's name in Paris. I am not French, as you know! As for his age, what made you place him in your mind as elderly?'

At this point I played what I felt to be my trump card. 'There are snow-white hairs adhering to the inside of the crown, quite a few of them. By the way, I deduce his height from his head size, which is six and seven eighths; it is my medical opinion based on personal experience that persons with such a head size are invariably tall and slight of build.'

'Oh, Watson, you are priceless! Let me give you an advanced lesson in the art of deduction. The owner of this hat may well have dwelt in America, but is not native to that country. He is probably quite young, and heavy of build. He may also be well below the average in height. Far from immaculate he is likely to be of somewhat careless appearance.'

I suppose I must have sounded a little sulky as I enquired, 'Would you care to substantiate these deductions?'

'To begin with, Watson, you have failed to notice that despite its head size the hat has been pulled down upon a head much larger than that for which it was intended. Notice the slackening of the stitches on the sweatband, which is stained, suggesting a heavy man who perspires even in moderate climes. The roll on the sides of the brim have been rolled even further, by hand, in the European style, a fashion not popular in New York. In order to emphasize this roll, the wearer has worried at the brim with his fingers, and you will notice that his rather lengthy nails have left their indentations. All of this somewhat belies your interesting character study of a tall, immaculate and somewhat elderly gentleman!'

'You have not explained about his age, or indeed, come to think of it, how you can tell regarding his theatre background.'

Sherlock Holmes was at his most irritating as he explained, 'There are indeed snowy-white hairs adhering to the inside of the crown, but let us examine them more carefully, Watson. Be so kind as to pass the tweezers from my bench.'

I brought him the tweezers and with them he extracted perhaps half-a-dozen hairs from the hat, then passing the headgear to me he carried the hairs to his microscope. He placed these upon a slide and looked through the eyepiece, turning the focus knob. Then he arose, clapped his hands, saying, 'As I thought . . . take a look for yourself, Watson!'

I examined the hairs through the incredible lens and recognized them for what they were. 'Animal hairs, Holmes, possibly those of a rodent, perhaps a white rat?'

He shook his head. 'The research that I made for a forthcoming monograph tells me that the hairs belong to a rabbit, probably of the Dutch variety. This breed would have been small enough to be inside the hat. Moreover, if you look more carefully you will find a few black hairs among the white ones, typical of the breed.'

The situation presented appeared ludicrous in the extreme and I expressed this with a question. 'Who on earth would allow a rabbit, Dutch or otherwise, to occupy his expensive silk hat?'

Holmes's answer was logical. 'A conjurer, Watson, which

tells us his profession; information to add to our belief in his general style and appearance. By the way, although quite young our visitor will be scant of locks. There are a few hairs upon the sweatband which are undoubtedly human and have been treated with a pomade designed to assist those with thinning hair.'

The new mantel clock, a gift from a grateful client, struck the hour, but it was several minutes past it before Mrs Hudson entered with a visiting card upon her tray. Holmes looked at it and read aloud to me, 'Horace Goldin. "The Whirlwind of Wizardry".'

Although the card was larger than that normally used in polite society it appeared to be of good quality but clearly flamboyantly theatrical.

Mr Goldin proved to be a plump young man, expensively if carelessly dressed. He wore no hat upon his dark though thinning head. His hands were plump and bejewelled, and his cravat was decorated with a jewelled stock-pin. In polite society he might have been thought to be overdressed and vulgar, yet his homely features bore a charming smile and his manner was charismatic. He spoke with a heavy accent which I could not quite place.

'Mr Holmes, I see you got my hat. I gotta mind like the boat with holes in it. I am Goldin, in person!'

He pronounced this last word the American way, to sound like a lethal draught!

Holmes introduced me. 'This is my friend and colleague, Dr John Watson, before whom you may speak freely. Pray be seated, Mr Goldin, and tell me what I may do for you.'

The charming little conjurer sat in our best armchair and tried to explain in halting, broken English, punctuated by the occasional American expression or intonation.

'Mr Holmes, Doctor, I am of course not English so forgive my way of speaking; I am from Russia . . . or Poland . . . or Lithuania. I cannot say which really, because I don't know which army occupied my town at the time of my birth. It was Vilnja and my family lived in the ghetto. But we got out of there and arrived in the United States when I was quite young. We lived in Nashville, in Tennessee, where we were treated rough, but nothing to how the Cossacks had treated us. When I was about eleven years old I saw a famous magician, Alexander Herrmann, and he pulled coins out of my ear and I wanted to do the same. When I left school I became first a store clerk for my uncle, but later still I went to Chicago where I got work as an act in vaudeville.'

At this point Holmes, so far extremely patient, interrupted. 'Mr Goldin, I find your life story fascinating, but does it have any bearing upon the problem you have desired to lay before me?'

Goldin was contrite and apologized.

'My dear Mr Holmes, I am so sorry, but just let me say that I struggled for years until I came to your country just a few months ago to appear at the Palace Theatre. I was a big success because I had original magic and I worked so fast . . .'

Holmes was starting to fidget again, but Goldin really did get to the point at last.

'But what made me really hit the big time was the fact that King Edward visited the theatre and enjoyed my act so much that he came again and again. Then he invited me to Sandringham, where he held a house party, to perform for his guests. The result was that the King gave me this stick-pin with diamonds and rubies, and at the theatre they extended my contract and started to bill me as The Royal Illusionist.'

Holmes was no longer impatient; the story of the private performances at Sandringham seemed to give him a feeling of something more urgent to come. Goldin sensed that he now had our attention and continued his narrative.

'Well, everything was fine until I got back to London. I heard that a very valuable painting was missing from the music-room at Sandringham. Now, Mr Holmes, I used that room to get ready for the show. You see, it opened onto the drawing-room so that I could get my things ready and make up my face and prepare. Other people were there of course but as a foreigner I figured that I might be suspected. I was questioned about it by an Inspector Lestrade from Scotland Yard, but he didn't give me too much trouble. However, I am in real trouble, Mr Holmes, for just when I have made it big in the theatre along comes something that could ruin me.'

I decided to venture a few words at this point. 'But surely, Mr Goldin, you know that you are innocent, so if no accusation has been made you have no need to worry.'

'If they do not find the real thief it could cast a dark shadow over me. Publicity like that I could do without.'

Holmes nodded his understanding and said, 'Mr Goldin, you wish me to investigate the matter and try to find the guilty party and, if possible, the painting?'

'Of course. And listen, I don't care how much it costs!'

'I have a set scale of charges, Mr Goldin, from which I do not make variation, save where I decide to make no charge at all.'

Goldin nodded. 'I understand; you are an English

gentleman. Pinkerton's would have cost me a fortune.'

Holmes rang for Mrs Hudson and ordered a pot of coffee, sensing that the longwinded Mr Goldin would take his time upon the details of his problem.

The plump little man fairly shovelled sugar into his coffee, saying, 'I like it sweet, it gives me energy; that and cigars. Do you mind if I smoke?'

Holmes charged his pipe from the Turkish slipper by way of answer and I offered Goldin a cigar from the scuttle. He chuckled over this unconventional resting place for the coronas and cut the end off one with a gold implement and lit it with one of these new contraptions that can be carried in the pocket to give a flame. I admired this and managed to talk him out of giving it to me. Then he picked up one of the small table napkins and rolled it between his palms. It got smaller and smaller and finally vanished entirely. He took a pack of cards from his pocket, fanned it and offered it to me to make a choice. I took one of the cards, which was the nine of clubs, and he bade me sign my name upon it. He folded it and rolled it into a small compass and caused it to vanish. Then he broke open the cigar which he was still smoking and extracted that rolled and folded card and opened it to reveal my name still signed upon it!

I was amazed, but Holmes coughed his impatience and Goldin took the hint. 'Inspector Lestrade told me that the robbery was quite a clever one. Someone had painted a copy of the picture and taken the real one from the frame, leaving the fake in its place.'

Holmes asked, 'Could this substitution not have been made days or even weeks before you came upon the scene?'

'That is what I hoped, but the inspector found out that the painting had been cleaned only the day before and by an expert who would have noticed the change.'

I asked, 'When was the substitution actually discovered?'

'The day after my performance. The expert had some extra polishing or something to carry out and of course found out that it was not the painting that he had cleaned.'

Holmes asked with interest, 'Did you say that it was a portrait?'

'Sure. Some German person, and I think the artist was called Rembrandt.'

Holmes whistled. 'Ah ha, an art treasure indeed, probably priceless. Whoever has stolen the painting can hardly sell it on the open market.'

'What, then, would he do with it and why did he steal it?' Goldin asked the very question that was in my mind.

Holmes's answer was precise. 'The painting was stolen for one of three reasons. The first upon the orders of some extremely eccentric collector who might keep such masterpieces in such a bizarre and secret setting that he alone might enjoy it. The second, the robber may be able to negotiate a ransom with the King for its safe return.'

He tailed off and I ventured to remind him, 'You have cited two examples, but you mentioned that there might be a third.'

'Yes. Sometimes, world-famous antiquities are stolen by those who do it from sheer bravado. Usually such whimsical criminals — if such they can be termed — return that which they have stolen. It is done just to prove that they can do it.'

'Which of the three reasons do you suspect?'

'Oh come, Watson, it is too early for me to express such an opinion; I need to know more, far more of the circumstances. I may need to visit the scene and examine the fake painting if it still hangs at Sandringham.'

'Will the King permit you to do so?'

'Quite possibly, for we did perform a service for him at about the time of his coronation. Indeed, Watson, you may remember that we made the very act of his crowning possible. Yet I would prefer it if the King knew nothing of our involvement; one can do so much more when incognito.'

Holmes questioned Horace Goldin a little further, and then quite suddenly he arose and announced that this interview was at an end. Goldin rose and nodded.

As I handed him his silk hat he grinned and said, 'This is the famous hat from which I produce my little Dutch rabbit. I picked it up in error. It does not fit my large head; it is used only as a magical property.'

As we shook hands with Goldin Holmes caught my eye. His deductions had been so accurate. The amiable magician handed us two squares of pasteboard. These bore the printed inscription, *Palace Theatre, Row A: number 21*. As might be surmised the second card bore the same message, save that it was numbered *22*. We thanked him politely and I wondered if Holmes would make use of these complimentary tickets.

Rather to my surprise my friend decided that we should attend a performance of the varieties presented at the Palace Theatre.

He waxed ironic, as was his habit. 'Come, my dear Watson. Why should we not attend a vaudeville performance? It would make a change for you from violin recitals and I could enjoy being spared yet another comic opera by Gilbert and Sullivan. You know, Watson, it is said that there was a lengthy period when Gilbert did not address a single word to his collaborator. I personally might have wished that they had never even met!'

Later, as we sat, wearing our tails, in the stalls at the Palace Theatre it occurred to me just how much more respectable the music-hall had become since being taken from its native taverns and civilized by impresarios like Edward Moss and Sir Oswald Stoll. The auditorium of the Palace, with its gleaming brass rails and expensive velvet furnishings, was so like the best of the legitimate theatres save for the content of the performance — not that there was anything amiss with the show itself. For those who were devotees of this style of entertainment it was probably of the very finest quality, to match its setting.

Mr Goldin did not appear until the second half of the two-part selection of variety acts. There were performing dogs, two red-nosed comedians who indulged in crosstalk, and a young woman who paraded in a man's evening suit, declaring in song that she was Fleet Street Freddie. A man in Scottish regalia told jokes and sang Highland ballads and was immensely popular with the audience. Two men in leotards performed upon a high trapeze and a young woman balanced upon an unsupported ladder and made suggestive comments as she did so.

Through this first half Sherlock Holmes sat with his head bowed and with an expression of abject misery upon his face.

After a lively intermission he brightened a little during the performance of a young lady who was what I believe is termed in vaudeville circles as a lightning cartoonist. Dressed in a splendid crimson velvet gown she drew frenetically upon large sheets of paper with thick coloured chalks. She began with political and celebrity portraits: Gladstone, Asquith, Joseph Chamberlain, Sir Henry Irving and George Bernard Shaw — flaming-red beard and all! She drew imitations of famous paintings, *The Stag at Bay* and *The Laughing Cavalier*. Finally, using a mirror as a spotlight, she picked out members of the audience and drew satirical likenesses of them. She interspersed all of this with merry quips and rather pointed remarks.

She went down very well with the audience and especially well with Sherlock Holmes, who said to me quietly, 'A charming exhibition of skill and entertainment, Watson.'

Two comical acrobats followed, and then there was Horace Goldin.

I had seen conjurers and magicians before. Indeed, both Holmes and I had often witnessed performances by Maskelyne and Devant at the Egyptian Hall. These had been extremely polite and lethargic affairs compared with the performance we were about to see. I have read since that Mr Goldin changed the whole character of magic as a performing art, performing as much necromancy in two minutes as the established great magicians would use in a half-hour offering. Time has played its tricks with my memory regarding Mr Goldin's performance as seen for the first time. Indeed, I have seen him perform so often through the years since that time that I tend to confuse one showing with another. However, I will try to reconstruct for the reader some kind of account of what we saw, or rather what we thought we saw, on that night in the November of 1902.

Where Devant had made his leisurely entrance and prepared for his first miracle, Goldin had performed his first wonder before he had reached centre-stage. From beneath a foulard he had produced a bowl from which rose very real and angry-looking flames. Then he placed a silk handkerchief upon the barrel of a rifle which he aimed at a glass decanter on a side-table. As the gun exploded, the hand-kerchief vanished from its barrel and suddenly appeared in the glass decanter. Four geese appeared from a seemingly innocent wooden tub and canaries placed in a paper bag were dematerialized to reappear in their cage. Goldin whipped away the cloth from a table without disturbing various vases, glasses and teacups that were upon it. He showed a top hat to be innocent, then, having wrapped a small rabbit in a sheet of paper, he tore it up with vigour, the rabbit's ears and head suddenly rising out of the top hat, to be hauled out kicking in a lively manner. Many, many silk flags were produced from a small drum, made from tambourine rings and tissue paper. This was climaxed by the sudden appearance of a huge Union Flag which practically covered the theatre backdrop. In all of these happenings, Goldin had been aided by three or four people, certainly two young ladies among them, who had played a part in enabling the Whirlwind Wizard to be just that. He had spoken no words but lively music had been played throughout. I had never seen such a fast and furious feast of legerdemain, and assumed that the big flag had been Goldin's finale. Nothing could have been further from the truth and the miracles were just about to commence.

After what seemed like a pause of no more than five seconds, Goldin further amazed his audience by catching goldfish from mid-air with a rod and line and depositing them in a bowl of water where they swam around in a lively manner. The magician entered a wire-fronted cage which was standing on a high pedestal whilst one of his female assistants stood in a small open-fronted cabinet. His male assistant put on a red cloak and a devil mask. This satanic character fired a pistol, causing the girl to vanish from the

17

cabinet. He fired at Goldin who vanished from the cage. Then to our amazement the girl ran down the centre aisle of the theatre towards the stage, and at almost the same moment the devil divested himself of his cloak and mask and proved to be Horace Goldin!

More miracles followed; for instance, the envanishment and reappearance of a fully-lit oil lamp. But the final theatrical effect was to knock everyone in the theatre for six.

The plump little magician held up his hands to the orchestra in order that they should cease to play. Then an assistant brought him a bedspread-sized cloth which Goldin held up in front of himself. After a second or two, the silence was broken by some four or five policemen rushing onto the stage, shouting and blowing whistles. These arms of the law stood around the cloth which Goldin was still holding in front of himself. There was a slow drum roll and suddenly a cymbal crash, as the cloth fell and the audience realized that Goldin had disappeared. The mild applause and reaction which greeted this feat showed how effective the previous miracles had been. But this gentle applause changed to gasps of astonishment and thunderous hand clapping as the principal policeman took off his hat and whiskers to reveal that he was Horace Goldin!

As the final strains of God Save the King died away, I turned to Holmes and asked, 'Well, Holmes, what do you make of friend Goldin now?'

He replied very quietly, 'He is a very amazing illusionist, Watson. In his offering there were items which I might almost term elementary; but there are aspects of his performance to worry even this jaded realist!'

One of Goldin's assistants gave us a message as we left our seats. We were invited to join the illusionist in his dressing-room as he had news for us. He led us to the stage door where we were admitted past the beady gaze of the stage doorkeeper. He took us beyond the iron staircases which led up to the dressing-rooms of the lesser artistes and through to the row of rooms which were handy to the wings and occupied by the principals.

The charming Horace Goldin made us most welcome, seating us and producing spirits and a gasogene bottle that we might refresh ourselves. As we sipped at our drinks and smoked his cigars he removed the florid theatrical make-up from his rubicund face. As he retreated behind a screen in order to change from his evening wear to his street clothes his voice continued to interact with our own speech.

'So, you enjoyed my performance, gentlemen?'

I decided to enthuse for us both, in case Holmes was in one of his strange moods. 'Your performance was enthralling; we were both entertained and mystified. I'll wager that my friend Holmes was as bewildered as I.'

Holmes all but snapped, 'Not quite, but let us say that I have seen things this evening that I cannot as yet explain.' He looked thoughtful, then continued, 'In fact, I would prefer not to apply my talents for deduction to your mysteries, Mr Goldin. It is so much nicer to think that there might still be a little magic in the world.'

Goldin emerged from behind the screen, wearing a suit which had probably cost him a great deal of money, but looked rather like the cover of a bed.

Holmes smiled as he spoke. 'You disappoint me, sir, for I had half expected the screen to collapse to reveal that you had vanished!'

I joined in with Goldin's dutiful laughter, but I knew that Holmes was anxious to know what Goldin's news could be.

I voiced this, trying as ever to play Holmes's diplomat (a role with which I had persisted through the years, despite occasional rebuffs).

'I believe you have some news for us, Mr Goldin.'

'Oh such news have I got! What do you think is in here?'

He produced an impressive-looking envelope.

Holmes replied with a surprisingly fast response. 'Could it be another invitation to perform for His Majesty?'

I cannot say that Goldin was amazed, in fact he nodded quietly and smiled like a cherub. 'You recognize the style of the envelope, but how did you know that it was another invitation to perform rather than an accusation?'

'My dear Goldin, an accusation would not have borne a crest upon its envelope, nor would that envelope have been so splendid. Indeed, Inspector Lestrade would probably have delivered it in person and, when he left, you would have gone with him. Tell me, are you alone among the company invited to appear or are other artistes involved?'

'Just as before, they want a couple of supporting acts. Last time I took the lightning artist and a singer. But the singer is no longer with the company so I thought I would take the Scotsman. I think I'll take the lightning artist again because she did well before and has a large repertoire. The King was delighted with her sketch of him and with those of some of his guests.'

Sherlock Holmes looked thoughtful and lowered his voice to enquire, 'Goldin, could you take us with you — Watson and I — as members of your company? You see, although the King would agree to our being present were I to request it, I would prefer that we should be there incognito; merging into the background so to speak. In that way we might be able to learn something that has been overlooked by Lestrade.'

I could not help but add, 'That would not be too diffi-cult!'

'My dear Watson, such remarks do not suit you.'

I grunted, and Goldin brightened as he felt that he had had a sensible suggestion.

'Mr Holmes, Doctor, you could come with me as assist-ants. If you were to wear workers' clothes, Dr Watson could shave his whiskers and you, Mr Holmes, could wear false ones!'

I fingered my moustache ruefully; it had been with me since my student days; but Holmes nodded our assent to the idea. 'A splendid thought, Goldin. But would we not require a great deal of rehearsal?'

'No time for that as the invitation is for this coming weekend. It is a house party, which I would not usually be able to stay for; but my engagement here finishes on Satur-day so I will be able to stay a day or two. Last time I had to go there by express train and come back overnight in an automobile. Even then, I had to miss one performance, but the management were so delighted to be able to advertise me as The Royal Illusionist that they did not mind. No, you will need no rehearsals; I'll just dress you as Arabs and you can bring things to me on trays. We can make your part in my act very small. Don't worry!'

Back at Baker Street we discussed our new careers over a late-night pipe by the fireside. The bellows brought up the dying embers to throw out some sort of heat.

I was a little apprehensive. 'Do you really think that the King will not suspect us or see through our disguises? After all, he has met both of us before.'

'Oh, I wouldn't let that worry you, Watson. The King is notoriously shortsighted, and he meets as many people in a day as you and I might in a month! No, that part of it will be easy, but as to whether we can discover anything of moment, well that is another story.'

I leaned over and pulled the bell to summon Mrs Hudson that I might request her to bring us some sandwiches of ham or some other cold meat which was always in good supply in her kitchen. In the continuance of our discussions concerning Horace Goldin's problem we were distracted to the extent that it was several minutes before we noticed that Mrs Hudson had not responded. I shrugged and pulled the bell again.

After a further three minutes had passed it was Holmes who remarked, 'Curious, Watson. I have excellent hearing so I know that the bell is responding to your manipulation of its cord; also I am aware that Mrs Hudson is at home as usual; moreover, Hudson has returned from his tavern for I detected the sounds of his key and his footsteps. Add to this the fact that Billy is almost certainly below stairs and we have a minor mystery on our hands. You have not, I suppose, upset the poor soul in some way?'

'Certainly not!' I was furious at his suggestion that I would ever treat the good lady with less than the courtesy which she at all times deserved. Indeed, I was about to remark that it was far more likely to be through some escapade of Holmes's, if indeed she had taken exception to something.

But he spoke before I could voice my thoughts. 'My dear fellow, I observe that you are made furious by my remark, which was in fact made in a jocular manner. Please accept my apology. Oh, and be so good as to investigate the basement that we might ascertain if something is amiss or adrift.'

I grunted as I rose to do as he requested, thinking how like Holmes it was to be so prompt to apologize where the fault was mine in being so quick to take offence where none had been intended. It was true to form also that he should suggest that it was I who should investigate a mundane domestic affair.

I coughed and tapped upon the partly-open basement parlour door. Receiving no response, I risked pushing the door fully open and entered the apartment.

The scene which greeted me filled my heart with dismay. For there was the good lady, seated with her head in hands, bowed over the table at which also sat the ruddy-faced Hudson, an expression of incomprehension upon his slightly intoxicated visage. Billy, for once very quiet and serious, also sat at the table, though unable to resist nibbling at a custard tart. However, as soon as I appeared it was Billy who leapt to his feet.

'Dr Watson, cor, 'scuse us but we ain't quite as we should be!'

I did not quite comprehend his meaning — or indeed that of Hudson as that worthy rose unsteadily to his feet.

'Ho, Doctor, don't often see yer down yere!'

I had to await a response from the good lady herself before I could begin to understand the situation which was making all three of them behave in a rather strange manner. She rose, a little unsteadily but not for the same reason as her husband. She had been crying as I could see from her tear-stained cheeks where little pale rivulets had attacked the rouge.

'Oh, Doctor, forgive Hudson and Billy, but we've had some bad news. Is there something I can do for you?'

'I rang, intending to request some sandwiches, Mrs Hudson; but if you have some problem please do not trouble yourself . . .' I trailed off, scarcely knowing what to say.

She was now remarkably composed again. 'Oh you rang and we were so concerned with our problems that we did not even hear it. Forgive me, I will make a plate of sandwiches, enough for yourself and Mr Holmes. I have a nice cold joint of beef that should be just the ticket, sir.'

I gently patted her shoulder and assured her of the lack of urgency for refreshments. 'Dear lady, the sandwiches can wait. Pray tell me of your problem that I might try to be of help with it. That is if it is not of too delicate a nature?'

She busied herself with the bread, butter and beef joint as she spoke. 'You are so kind, Doctor, but I think there is nothing that anyone can do. You see this house, which I have occupied for quite some years as you know, is what they call Crown property. I took a lease on it many years ago, being told at the time that when that lease expired I would almost certainly be able to renew it on very similar terms. I have never infringed any of the conditions of the lease, neither have any of my tenants; though Mr Holmes has come near to it a few times. I thought it would all be a foregone conclusion as I think you might call it.'

I thought I comprehended her problem. 'I see, and for some reason, your lease having expired, the Crown estates will not renew it. Has any reason been given?'

'Yes, sir. The Crown wishes to build some sort of municipal building upon the site of this and several adjoining buildings which they own. I've got six months to vacate the premises! Oh me, what is a body to do, and what am I going to tell Mr Holmes?' She could hold the tears back no longer.

I comforted her as best I could. 'There, there, dear lady. Holmes can look after himself, as can I. It is only your good self we have to worry about. Holmes and I have a few people that we could contact with a view to finding you another residence on similar terms. Why, who knows, perhaps you could then let rooms to Holmes and me, and life could slowly arrive back at something like normality.'

She shook her head. 'I fear not, Dr Watson. I will never be able to raise the money for another lease.'

There was not a lot more I could say that would be of comfort to the poor woman so I slipped away, having been told that the sandwiches would be sent up to us very shortly. As I returned to our sitting-room I wondered just how I would break the news to Holmes who was sitting upon the floor poring over a map.

He looked up at me and spoke in a rather distracted manner.

'Watson! I had no idea how extensive and complicated the surrounding area of Sandringham House could be.'

I wanted to tell him at once about Mrs Hudson's problem but had to await my chance.

'Why there are vaults and all manner of ornate summer houses, not to mention outbuildings for the storage of marquees and things of that sort.'

I tried to interrupt. 'Holmes, Mrs Hudson has had some bad news . . .'

He sighed as he placed the map aside. 'You mean the fact that her lease is not to be renewed?'

'She has told you about it? She gave me the impression that she had kept it to herself until now!'

'Watson, the poor soul has told me nothing, I just deduced as much.'

'I fail to see how you could have unless you have added second sight to your repertoire!'

'Oh come, Watson, I already knew of the fact that this building was Crown property, and recently noticed the presence in Baker Street of Crown surveyors with their tape measures and other paraphernalia. Have you not noticed a chalk mark upon the pavement on the northern side of this property indicating a boundary? Add to this a marked gloomy air upon the part of both Mrs Hudson and Billy. I can tell you, when the good lady failed to answer your ring for the first time that I can remember, I realized the full implications. However, I have other matters to concern me at present.'

I could scarcely believe his cavalier attitude towards the landlady's problems. My anger at this quite stopped any admiration I may have held for the skill of his deductions. But when Mrs Hudson herself appeared with the repast where I had expected to see Billy, Holmes was kindness itself and spoke to her in a manner which made me at once feel that, not for the first time, I had misjudged my friend.

'Ah, Mrs Hudson. I have learned something of your problems.' He gave no indication of just how he had learned of them, leaving her to assume that I alone had broken the bad news. 'But let me assure you that when our present pressing investigations are completed I will give my best attention to being helpful to you. Come, dear lady, we have been together a long time, and whilst all good things must come to an end I have a feeling that in this instance the end is not yet in sight!'

Where my commiserations had been of little help and effect, Holmes, with a few well-chosen words, managed to lift the cloud from the brow of the poor woman. I felt that

I had been hasty in my previous thoughts concerning his attitude. She left the room with hope.

I turned to commend his words but he brushed my remarks aside and pointed to the map — which he had taken up again — with the stem of his pipe.

CHAPTER TWO

Sandringham House

I had travelled in a motor-car only once before, so I was a little apprehensive when we piled into the huge Daimler which bore the royal crest upon its doors. It was upon the Saturday night, after Goldin's final performance at the Palace, and we travelled by road as the train would not have been able to get us to King's Lynn in time for the command performance, which evidently was to take place upon the following day. Goldin explained to us that he had decided to take a monologist instead of the Scottish singer, music being frowned upon on Sunday at Sandringham.

He said, 'Madame Francis will still be suitable because she can do her act without music. I can manage too, but it's more difficult for me because I will need to talk as music is forbidden. My English is terrible as you know, and I only hope the King and Queen will forgive it.'

It was a long journey, but smooth enough thanks to the luxurious royal motor-car. Goldin had his two young lady assistants, Dolly and Milly, with him as well as us. Also present were Madame Francis and the monologist who introduced himself as Arthur Hale. He was a pale-skinned man with a mournful face; plump, but not quite a rival to Goldin in that respect. Madame Francis proved to be an amiable enough lady, but rather on her dignity when compared with the giggling sisters — as Goldin described Dolly and Milly.

In the seat which opened out at the back of the vehicle sat a footman, though not in powdered wig and finery. Finally, Dobson the chauffeur completed the group. It was rather too late to stop for refreshment anywhere, but the King had been kind enough to supply a hamper with cold meat and champagne.

Holmes quite managed to merge into the background in his tweed suit which was a trifle small for him, plus an extremely well-made and realistic false moustache. It was one of a collection which he had made himself from his own hair. Minus my faithful upper-lip adornment, I fancied I looked very strange indeed. Goldin had named us Smith and Jones — after an undertaker's sign that I once had seen.

Of course the reader will understand that Goldin during this journey could speak to us only as he would to a couple of newly-hired assistants. This presented us with no problems because his manner with his employees was as polite as it was with others. But it did mean that we could not bring up the subject of the missing painting. But Horace Goldin kept us entertained with an incredible repertoire of magical feats. He showed us card tricks that were rare in that they were not boring, produced articles from our hats which we knew had never been there before and he performed some thought-reading experiments which particularly intrigued Madame Francis and Arthur Hale. Milly and Dolly had doubtless seen it all before but there were moments when even they became animated in their interest.

It was a long journey but it passed remarkably quickly. In fact — as Goldin reproduced a coin that I had lent him from one of the bread rolls, having made it dematerialize by dropping it into a glass of champagne — I was rather surprised to learn that we had reached the very gates of Sandringham House.

Of course, Goldin's graphic accounts of his own experience previously had helped to make us less wide-eyed than might otherwise have been the case when we entered the Royal Household. Goldin, Madame Francis and Arthur Hale were taken straight in through the stately front entrance, whilst Milly, Dolly, Holmes and I were escorted to the staff quarters by an assistant butler. It was late, but the staff took us to the kitchen where they treated us with great kindness and brought us bread and cheese and tankards of ale.

One of the kitchen maids — of the sort which in a lesser menage would have been called a skivvy — was still hard at work polishing silver cutlery.

She smiled at us and said, 'Must have it all ship-shape for their Majesties' luncheon tomorrow.'

We nodded and smiled.

Holmes remarked to me, very softly, 'I observe that the King's cousin, Wilhelm, will be present.'

'The Kaiser? I had no idea that he was to be present and I fail to see how you can know this.'

'Fail to see! Exactly, you have failed to notice the extra long dining forks that do not match the other cutlery.'

Of course, Holmes's gimlet eyes had taken in these rather strange-looking forks at a glance. I grasped now how his deduction had been made. He knew, as did I, that the Kaiser had a malformation to his left arm, making his reach shorter than normal. His manipulation of dining cutlery was made easier for him by the use of these long-handled forks. Despite intermittent tension at political and military levels the Kaiser had always been a regular visitor to the royal households, just as Teddy was welcome in the palaces of the great Austro-Hungarian Empire.

The assistant butler, or under-butler as he was probably better known, Walshingham, joined us at the table and proved to be an amiable enough fellow.

'Smith and Jones, eh? Sounds like a firm; bookmakers, undertakers, I even knew a couple of bailiffs called Smith and Jones! They weren't after my goods and chattels; just those of my employer.'

I put my foot in it by asking, 'Surely the King did not have debts, even when he was the Prince of Wales?'

Holmes kicked me under the table but the under-butler took my remark quite casually,

'Concerning his Majesties' financial affairs, my lips are sealed, Mr Jones; though I could tell you a tale or two. But no, I was previously employed by a noble earl who was greatly taken with the sport of kings. In fact he lost all his money on them, the horses that is, what he had not already lost at the gaming tables or at the casinos in Monte Carlo.'

Holmes tried to direct him gently towards the subject of the missing Rembrandt. 'I imagine you also need to be diplomatic concerning the missing painting.'

'Oh, so you know about that? Well, there is no harm then in talking to you about it. You are not a journalist in disguise are you?'

Holmes chuckled, 'I give you my word that I am not a journalist. My friend and I have also been advised to observe discretion upon the subject. But it is a serious matter, is it not?'

'Indeed it is, Mr Smith, and whilst I understand how it was done, I know not by whom and quite how it was managed.'

'You refer to the substitution of a copy of the portrait?'

'Why yes, that was a clever ruse, and it needed an even smarter one to get the real painting out of here. Why, even your guv'nor's traps were frisked before he left, though I don't think he even knew that it happened. The same can be said about the other artistes that had come with him. The other guests were all titled people, and the staff here are beyond reproach; it's a family business, Mr Smith, if you know what I mean?'

I dared to interject an enquiry. 'I suppose no tradesmen were about at the time when the picture was stolen?'

'Not in that part of the building, Mr Jones. Deliveries are at this end, and there were no builders about during that period. Inspector Lestrade has been all over that anyway, so no point in any of us worrying.'

It was late, very late, and we were not sorry to lay our heads upon the royal pillows, even if these were of the kind intended for those in service, but of course we inevitably discussed that which we had so far seen and heard.

'As far as I can see, Watson, there was a rather short period of time during which the thief could exchange the portraits and abscond with the real one.'

'You mean that your first task is to discover just when the room was unoccupied, leaving the field clear for the theft?'

'Yes. I am also anxious to notice the reactions to the

inevitable winding down of the investigation. I must confer with Lestrade on the morrow.'

This meeting did indeed come about upon the morrow, but at an even earlier time than we had expected. We were taking an early-morning stroll in the grounds when we came upon Lestrade and his sergeant. For a moment the good inspector did not recognize us, and chuckled quietly when eventually he did. He was even more amused when he learned the nature of our disguise.

'Well, well, a new calling for you, Mr Holmes or, rather, Mr Smith. I always did think of you and the doctor as tricky customers, but magician's assistants, eh! Seriously, though, what do you make of this Goldin fellow?'

Holmes's answer was spoken with great sincerity. 'My calling has made me a good judge of character and in my opinion he is as straight as a die.'

I nodded my assent but Lestrade seemed a little in doubt.

'I'm not so sure; he is a foreigner, you know, and a tricky customer at that. Why, do you know he lifted my watch, even if he did return it to me very smartly.'

I remarked, 'Come, Lestrade, he is a trickster by profession, is he not? After all, J N Maskelyne is a substantial citizen, not to mention young Devant.'

Lestrade replied, 'You may be right, Doctor, but it does seem rather rum that a man who is a deceiver by profession should be present at the very time of the disappearance of a priceless painting.'

Holmes suggested, 'You do not then give any suspicious thought to others? For example, those whom Goldin brought with him?'

'They have all been questioned, of course; the two girls, both scatterbrained Americans, are not bright enough to indulge in such a dangerous enterprise, unless . . .' he lowered his voice, 'unless it is under the skilled direction of their employer.'

'How about Madame Francis?'

'The Frenchwoman? I think not, but if she took it she certainly did not remove it from the premises. All of the artistes' property was examined, even if they were unaware of it. They were all checked out again when they left Sandringham House. You see, the theft had already been discovered before then and I was on the scene.'

'How about the guests and staff of His Majesty?'

'Nothing can be ruled out, Mr Holmes, but it seems unlikely that any of the lords or ladies are candidates for a Raffles job! As for the staff, they have security for life, are paid more than most of their kind and live always as well as their masters. But, as I say, nothing can be ruled out.'

Lestrade joined us for breakfast in the servants' dining-room. This was by no means taken in as relaxed an atmosphere as had been our repast of the night before. To begin with, the very presence of a detective inspector produced a subdued air among the staff, and also the fact that Lestrade could not confer with us save in our new personae of Smith and Jones made converse more difficult.

Walshingham caused us to be served just as if we were at the royal breakfast table but was, of course, himself a little more relaxed than he would have been in the royal presence.

Lestrade enquired of him, 'Is everyone that you are expecting here, Mr Walshingham?'

'Why yes, inspector, save for the Germans. You know, sir,

those who came with his Germanic Majesty.' He lowered his voice as if the presence of the Kaiser was still a secret, although I felt sure that it was not.

Eventually the Germans put in an appearance. There were three of them, two men and a middle-aged woman. All three were wooden-faced and sat stiffly at the table, looking with suspicious glances at all that was set before them. They were offered the same courses as ourselves but did not seem to accept them with the same relish. But then I was never one to turn my nose up at a big plateful of sausage, eggs, bacon, kedgeree and liver. Indeed, I made such a good stab at it that I scarcely had room for the toast and preserves which followed it. It is no reflection upon Mrs Hudson, who always kept a good table, when I say that I felt that I was living like a king; well, certainly as far as the inner man was concerned.

'Is the staff group not a small one for the King and Queen of Prussia?' My enquiry was a subdued one, made to Walshingham.

The under-butler replied, 'It is an unofficial visit, Mr Jones. Were it official there would be a small army of servants and guards; I would count it a personal favour if you were to implore the rest of your party not to mention this second royal presence until their majesties are safely home.'

I agreed to use my influence but this was scarcely required because it fell to the lot of Inspector Lestrade to do this officially. He gathered us together and read us the riot act — as we used to say in the army. 'None of you is to breathe a word about the Kaiser being here. I have enough trouble over this stolen picture without having any international incidents to worry about.'

Of course, the reader will realize that the horrific events which began in 1914 were still undreamed of. Indeed, another decade was to have passed before the outbreak of the Great War. Yet even so, a certain tension was building up in Europe. The Kaiser was still popular with most British people, with our working classes referring to him — almost affectionately — as Willie, much as they called the King Teddy. But of course there are maniacs everywhere and all rulers have their enemies.

An hour or so later we were in the music-room which, despite the recent theft from its walls, was again to be used to serve the drawing-room in its use as a small theatre. As we each donned a tarboosh and djellaba, Holmes took the opportunity to examine the copy which hung in place of the missing Rembrandt. Nudging me, he spoke in a whisper to avoid being overheard by a footman in livery who stood stiffly beside the painting. (Though why he stood there I will never know, for there was little point in guarding the imitation!) 'I once saw the original, Watson, when it was on loan to a national exhibition. I am, as you well know, reasonably observant but I feel that it would be difficult to detect the difference.'

Goldin bustled in and placed the items which he needed us to handle onto a number of trays. Each bore a number written upon gummed paper which he had stuck to the trays. 'I clap my hands, and shout, "Jones, tray number one, please" and so on. Very easy for clever guys like you. Usually, as I said before, I don't say anything as there is music. Today, I must talk.'

The royal party had returned from church and partaken of lunch and were already seated in rows in the drawing-room. I chanced a quick peep round the door and saw the awe-inspiring sight of our Monarch and his Queen seated in throne-like chairs. Alongside them, in scarcely less splendid chairs, sat the Kaiser and his consort.

Madame Francis opened the programme with her brilliant lightning cartoons and sketches. She made a wonderful caricature of the Kaiser, drew some political figures, evidently different to those she had presented on her previous Sandringham appearance and finally she sketched some wonderful woodland scenes and seascapes with coloured chalks. As an encore she was requested to repeat her lightning drawing of His Majesty. She accompanied it all with a rapid patter in broken English to compensate for the lack of musical background that she had enjoyed at the music-hall and at Sandringham on her earlier showing. As she made an exit, as graceful as a woman carrying an easel can make, she breathed a sigh of relief and deposited her properties near to the questioned portrait.

Holmes, in his Smith guise, spoke to her in a friendly fashion. 'Your English is remarkable, madame, but I trust you will not lose that delightful French accent. I believe you were here when the Rembrandt was stolen. As an artist what do you make of this substituted copy?'

He indicated the painting in its frame and she smiled at him bewitchingly as she replied, 'You are too kind about my English. As for my opinion of the picture, I imagine it must have been exchanged whilst I was actually performing. I went out into the gardens immediately after, so I did not hear of the theft until I returned.'

I could not resist making an enquiry at this point. 'A stroll, all alone, madame?'

She shot me a sharp glance and Holmes shot me an even sharper one. But she was polite in her reply, 'It was a meeting, a . . . how can I put it — an assignation, sir — I had promised a certain gentleman that I would promenade with him. I am afraid I cannot divulge the gentleman's name.'

Holmes quickly used some diplomacy. 'My dear lady, I have no wish to pry, neither, I feel sure, had my colleague. We were merely making conversation.'

We did not see Horace Goldin again until we were enlisted to carry trays to him, bearing the impedimenta of illusion. When the major-domo announced him he was in fact seated in the audience, near the back of the room. When announced he rushed down to the performing area and endeared himself to the audience with his breathless manner and fractured English. Of course, on the music-halls he is what I understand to be known as a silent act, but on this occasion he proved to be just as effective when he spoke, which he had to do as there was no musical accompaniment.

Goldin beckoned to me and I entered, holding the tray marked number one. He turned me so that I faced the audience and he started to extract eggs from my mouth, which he deposited upon the tray.

As he did this Goldin kept up a constant chatter. 'This is Abdul, I used to keep hens but now I just keep Abdul. He thinks he is a chicken. A doctor has offered to cure him of this but I cannot have that because I need the eggs! But I expect you wonder where the eggs are really coming from. Well, I will show you.'

He pulled the fez from my head and showed the audience that it was empty. Then, as much to my amazement as that of the assembled company, he produced from it a cackling, flapping, live bantam. I suppose he must have had it concealed about his person and had somehow managed to introduce it into the fez but I did not see him do so and neither, I imagine, did the audience. There was a roar of surprise and a burst of applause from the spectators who had, until that point, been somewhat subdued.

Then Goldin pushed me gently in the direction of the music-room door, at the same time snatching from the tray a small black cloth bag and one of the eggs that I had evidently disgorged.

It would be difficult to describe accurately what happened next but in essence Goldin made the egg vanish from the bag and then made it come back. The audience thought that they detected his ruses, only to find that they had merely observed that which they had been intended to. The King was inveigled into taking part and was allowed to examine the bag. Then, whilst he held the conjurer's wrists, the egg was reproduced. There was a gasp from the ladies as Goldin removed his tailcoat in order to show that there was nothing concealed about his person.

They applauded his brilliant manoeuvres with that elusive little egg. Finally it was Holmes's turn to carry a tray bearing various properties. Goldin took a glass goblet from the tray and extracted a number of gold coins from the air, dropping them into the goblet where they made a merry clink. Yet when he tossed them from the goblet into the air they had changed to a shower of metallic confetti. Then, as a finale, the enterprising little performer produced strings of silken flags from an extremely small tube. I was summoned to help, as were Milly and Dolly, and he wound us all in a silken blaze of colour.

The initially-stiff audience cheered, roared and applauded

the plump little Pole, as he took bow after bow. Eventually, the monologist commenced his turn but got little attention from the audience who were still enthralled by what Horace Goldin had shown them.

Back in the music-room, Horace was somewhat dismayed by the effect that he had on a fellow performer's act. He walked up and down and made clucking noises as the audience refused to give this artist their full attention. When the monologue finished and another was about to be commenced there was an interruption.

King Edward jumped to his feet and all but shouted, 'Excellent. Bravo. And now to make this a really splendid afternoon, Mr Goldin will show us some more of his wonders!'

There was an outbreak of cheering. Goldin looked at me and grinned ruefully, shot his linen and adjusted his waistcoat and rushed back into the fray. I wondered if he might have perhaps exhausted his repertoire, or at least that of it which he had brought with him. I remarked as much to Milly who just made a dismissive gesture with one hand.

She invited us to join her and Dolly for a stroll.

As the two girls went to fetch their cloaks I was amazed that Holmes had agreed to be party to such an enterprise. But he had his reasons for having agreed to it.

'Remember, they came here before with Goldin and were present when the theft took place. Moreover, Watson, we have had no chance for a thorough look around the grounds without seeming to show too much interest. Quite aside from that, a widower like yourself should really be seeking female company!'

I pretended to ignore his last words on the subject and resisted the temptation to make any allusion to his own bachelor status. Then, as the two American ladies joined us, they slipped their arms through ours and we emerged into the Sandringham grounds.

I would not wish the reader to think me unkind, but I am forced to say that as Sherlock Holmes walked arm in arm with Dolly he really did look the picture of misery: perhaps his drooping false moustache lent some air of melancholy to him but I could not commiserate as he had undertaken this enterprise with his eyes wide open.

Milly nudged me and placed her hand into my coat pocket where she found mine and squeezed it.

She said, 'Let's leave those two to themselves.'

She gave me no alternative and walked off in a different direction to theirs. Indeed, as we went through the business, she started to ask me a number of questions about Holmes and myself which I felt forced to answer but could only hope that Dolly was not similarly interrogating Holmes, or if she was that he and I would invent similar falsehoods.

'You and your pal: is Mr Goldin taking you on as part of the act?'

I thought quickly. 'Well, no, we were just taken on for this affair. We were medical students together . . . many years ago but we both failed our examinations. Since then we have taken on all manner of odd jobs.'

Milly raised her pencilled eyebrows.

Suddenly, there was a rustle in the bushes and I decided to take action. I grabbed Milly's arm and pulled her into the undergrowth in the opposite direction from whence the sounds had come. To my surprise I found that the bushes were concealing, or rather had concealed from us, a sort of stone edifice with a partly open door. I pushed the door which, although it was heavy, moved enough for me to see inside the building to some extent. Milly squeaked with excitement at the discovery and followed me as I made a tentative attempt to enter.

'What is this place?' Milly enquired.

'It is some sort of crypt.'

'You, you mean there are dead people in here?'

I glanced around at the big stone sarcophagus which was the centrepiece of the apartment and at some lesser versions of it which made corner pieces.

I answered Milly's question. 'Very possibly these stone resting places still contain remains. But this place may no longer be visited, even completely forgotten as it has obviously long been hidden by undergrowth. We may be the first persons to enter it for half a century.'

I had based this opinion on the labyrinth of cobwebs and moss that had settled on everything.

However, Milly seemed to have different views. 'Apart from the woman who came here recently and left her umbrella.' She indicated a rolled umbrella which leaned against the wall in a corner.

I replied, 'The umbrella is plain enough for it to have belonged to a man.'

But Milly showed surprising brightness of intellect for one that I had taken to be rather shallow. 'A man who wore girl's boots?'

My eyes followed her extended finger and I perceived that there were indeed prints in the moss and dust of ages that could only really have been made by a lady's boots, albeit rather large ones.

As we retreated back to the path I looked for the woman's footprints but could see none. However, it was Milly who discovered that the prints were there, two sets made by the same boots, running in opposite directions, but hidden from view with leaves and soil. I made a mental note to introduce Milly to Sherlock Holmes as soon as the circumstances would make this politic!

There was no sign of the others so we strolled back in the direction of Sandringham House. I managed to arrange it so that Holmes and I walked together just a few paces ahead of the two girls.

'Did Dolly ask you any awkward questions, Holmes?'

'One or two, Watson, including what our connection might be and where we had been previously employed.'

'Milly was equally curious on those points. I told her that we had both been medical students but had failed our examinations.'

'I told Dolly that you were a failed veterinarian and I was a bookmaker's runner!'

I was dismayed and could only hope that the two young ladies were finding other topics for discussion. Then I told Holmes about the umbrella and the tracks of a woman's size six boots, carefully disguised.

He was extremely interested in what I told him and said, 'My dear Watson, we will make a detective of you yet!'

I was about to tell him that it was Milly who had made the discoveries, but considering that it might complicate the issue I decided not to do so.

The night, which was to be our last at Sandringham House, was disturbed for me when Sherlock Holmes gave me a rough shake. He was fully dressed and minus his Smith disguise.

He hissed at me, 'The game is afoot, Watson. It is time for us to follow up your discoveries concerning the crypt.'

CHAPTER THREE

The Mystery of the Crypt

I led Sherlock Holmes to the spot where I knew the bushes were concealing that strange little crypt that I had told him about. By the light of his lantern we examined those trails which, although once covered, could be seen to lead in both directions: in and out. Alongside were the prints left in the soft ground by Milly and me. Holmes covered them again with loam and leaf mould, making a more professional job of it than I ever could have.

He remarked, 'We will cover our own tracks when we leave.'

We entered the crypt and I was struck by how even more bizarre the place appeared by the light of the dark lantern which threw strange shadows against the stark stone walls.

At first, Holmes seemed far more interested in the sarcophagus than in the umbrella, which I was relieved to see still leant against the wall in the corner. He pointed to the build-up of moss and stone fungi which surrounded the edges of the great stone lid where the supporting area was slightly wider.

'Judging by this natural build up I would say that it had not been necessary to open this place since 1864.'

I started, for although I knew his methods I could not see how they could give him such an accurate date assessment.

I said as much and brought forth an answering chuckle. 'With my lens I have read the date of his interment. I see no reason to think from the appearance of the rim that there has been any change in forty years. After all, his wife is no doubt among those encased in the smaller sarcophagi.

He transferred his attention to the inscription on one of these.

'Ah yes, she survived him by ten years. The family name was Battenburger. Possibly rather distant relatives to His Majesty.'

'What makes you say distant?'

'Were he close this crypt would not be hidden away as it is. In fact this very concealment leads me to think that Herr Gustave Battenburger was either a poor or embarrassing relative as well as being a distant one.'

As was so often his way, Holmes tried my patience by seeming to ignore the umbrella, which I felt must be significant. Instead of examining it he insisted upon giving me the value of his architectural and historical knowledge in describing the crypt. But at last he came to what I felt was the main point of our nocturnal visit.

'So, we come now to the presence of this ladies' umbrella.'

'It is not of either male or female style, Holmes. It could have been brought here by a man, one of the gardeners perhaps?'

'A gardener with a taste in ladies' size six boots?'

I had to admit that this information had first been pointed out to him by myself and I could hardly argue further. I just watched as he picked up that which was certainly an umbrella and not a parasol.

He held it up and asked, 'What do you make of it, Watson, giving regard to its general appearance and shape?'

'It is rolled, neatly enough, so I assume the owner is of neat habits.'

He studied it carefully and finally made his pronouncement.

'It is a fake, Watson, the thing is rolled but as wide near the ferrule as it is near the top. Look carefully and you will notice that its black silk shows no trace of the shapes that the ribs would make. Study the top and you will see that there is nothing to show the rib extremities, which would normally be in full view, capped by metal beads. The top is held together by a circle of black elastic. At a glance it may well resemble a rolled umbrella — albeit a very stout one.'

I studied it and could detect those points to which he had drawn my attention.

I enquired, 'But why would anyone make something to look like an umbrella when it is nothing of the kind?'

Holmes chuckled. 'I'll wager friend Goldin has owned such an object in his time. But I doubt that this belongs to him. As to its purpose, I imagine it has been constructed to conceal, or form a hiding place, for another object.'

'You mean like a swordstick?'

'Exactly! As to just what it conceals, well I will give you the legendary three guesses as to what we might find in this umbrella, Watson.'

'You mean the missing Rembrandt?'

'Such I believe will prove to be so. Hold the lantern, Watson, if you would be so good, whilst I investigate further.'

Sherlock Holmes peeled down the silken sleeve so that it rolled towards the ferrule, revealing what indeed appeared to be a tightly rolled canvas. As he unfurled it the reverse side was gradually revealed and there was no denying the strong possibility of it being the original of the copy which hung in the Sandringham House music-room. He took his lens to it, and paid particular attention to the signature.

'Almost certainly it is the missing Rembrandt. Notice the fake umbrella was made to accommodate it, with a very thin centre column of metal, and a length which is a little beyond normal expectation. The perpetrator of the theft must have brought the copy here by this same means of concealment, cut this original from its frame and made the substitution. Notice the edges, Watson. They have been recently cut, probably with a sharp knife rather than with a folding razor. Notice how a continuous cut has been largely managed; a razor would have required the work to be done with a series of shorter cuts.'

The discovery of the missing painting itself, however, quite overrode my interest in the details he expounded.

I enquired, 'Shall you take it straight to the King?'

He replied smartly, 'By no means, Watson. We will, however, take the umbrella with its concealed masterpiece, back to the house and conceal its existence.'

'Will you not alert Lestrade?'

'Tomorrow. Let him get his beauty sleep; in fact, let everyone concerned sleep the sleep of the blameless or the guilty, as may be their particular case.'

I admit that however much may be upon my mind and whatever the excitement to be faced upon the morrow I am invariably able to sleep the sleep of the blameless, as Holmes had put it. On this occasion I slept almost at once and awoke refreshed, if a little late for breakfast in the servants' hall.

No doubt had I been late for breakfast with their majesties' guests my tardiness would have been overlooked. No such allowance was made by the good Mr Walshingham.

He shook a finger at me. 'Mr Jones, I can only offer you bread and cheese or toast and preserve . . . everything else has been cleared away. But in any case, sir, I understand that your employer wishes to speak with you. I have already alerted Mr Smith who promptly left for the east wing; he asked me to alert you.'

I was directed to a small room in the east wing where Goldin and Holmes were seated at a table. Holmes was again in his disguise as Smith; without my moustache I, of course, had to play Jones no matter whether I liked it or not. That hirsute adornment to my upper lip had shared most of my adult life, so I still felt all but naked without it. In the army an officer without a moustache would have been unthinkable, and since those days, whilst it was not exactly a social bloomer to be clean shaven, such lack of whiskers would usually be remarked upon, making one stand out in a crowd; the last thing that a gentleman was expected to do.

Horace Goldin was rubbing his plump hands together and his rubicund face was wreathed in a smile. He beamed at me but waited for the servant who had directed me to make an exit before he spoke.

'Doctor Watson,' (he had, as ever, difficulty in speaking my name as starting with a W; the V usually found its way there), 'Mr Holmes has given me the great news already! So I am in the open as you might say?' He meant, no doubt, 'in the clear'.

I replied to the effect that I was also more than delighted with the turn that things had taken and that modesty forbade me from claiming more than passing credit for the discovery of the missing portrait.

Then Goldin dropped a minor bombshell.

'His Majesty has requested one final short performance before we go. I have been begging Mr Holmes to hold up his making his findings public until that is concluded, and to include it in the finale!'

I could see the direction that the magician's mind was taking; the restoration of the priceless Rembrandt putting the icing on the cake and the greatest piece of showmanship to climax anything in his career to date. Of course, Sherlock Holmes, although he had never been connected with the theatre, had a touch of the showman too. I had only to remember his presentation of the final revelations in the affair at Baskerville Hall to realize this. I had spent enough years with him to know from his expression and suppressed air of excitement that he had a suggestion or two for Goldin in this matter.

In its due place in this narrative the reader will discover just what Holmes and Goldin planned for the entertainment, and restoration of property to the King.

In our by now familiar roles as Smith and Jones we assisted Goldin as before, wearing our Arabian robes and headgear. We performed our easy tasks of fetching and carrying the trays, which bore yet another selection from the Polish magician's capacious repertoire.

The audience, by the way, was of a more intimate nature, with most of the lords, nobles and their ladies having departed. This left the King, Queen Alexandra, the Prince and Princess of Wales, the Kaiser and Kaiserine, Inspector Lestrade, and a mere handful of others. A small but enthusiastic gathering. The Kaiser seemed particularly delighted with Goldin's card tricks, and punctuated each revelation of a selected ace or queen with cries of 'Hoch, mein Gott!'

King Edward was also enthusiastic, especially when Goldin smashed his diamond ring with a hammer, made the fragments disappear from a cone fashioned from a newspaper, only to produce the ring, completely restored, from the innermost of a nest of boxes.

As the ring was returned to him the King remarked, rather ruefully I thought, 'By Jove, Goldin, pity you can't find a way to restore to me my missing Rembrandt, what?'

He looked around among his cronies, who laughed politely as soon as they realized that the remark was intended to be humorous and that it was politic to do so.

Goldin put down the piece of apparatus that he had intended to use and held up his hands as if calling for silence from a hilarious multitude rather than the polite titters of a dozen or so people.

He spoke, with his inimitable Polish-American accent. 'Your Majesty and Mrs Queen, and all the rest of you what came out of the top drawer. It would take more than my magic to make possible what your Majesty requests. It would take a great detective, and there perhaps I can help. Smith, Jones, stand to attention and I will try and transform the pair of you so that you become persons that could help with our problem!'

As we had rehearsed, Holmes and I stood stiffly to attention whilst Milly and Dolly came upon the scene and held before us a cloth of bedspread proportions. There was a hidden bag suspended on our side of the cloth, into which we deposited our robes and headgear. Beneath these robes we had been wearing, on this occasion, clothes rather like those which we would have worn had we been in Baker Street rather than the mufti we had effected as Smith and Jones. Thus we were ourselves again but for a few minor details.

Holmes tore off the moustache that had been glued to his upper lip and passed it to me. I took from my pocket a small phial of spirit gum, which I applied to the silken portion on the non-hairy side of the object. I applied it to my recently shorn upper lip to which, with a little pressure, it adhered. Of course, it was not exactly like the moustache that I had sacrificed, but it would do for our purpose.

Whilst this was happening, Goldin was pattering away in his quaint manner to keep the audience amused. Then, when we were ready, Holmes stamped his foot loudly to give the signal of readiness that we had arranged.

I think Goldin was relieved to hear it and he said, 'Please, will someone name a detective, other than the eminent Inspector Lestrade, whom they think might be able to solve this mystery which has been such an embarrassment to me and a worry to His Majesty?'

There were cries for Rodney Stone and other fictional sleuths such as Sexton Blake.

But it was the King himself who voiced the words that we were hoping to hear.

'What about jolly old Sherlock Holmes and his chum, Watkins, is it?'

It was Lestrade who corrected him. 'Dr Watson, Your Majesty.'

'By Jove, that's right. Sherlock Holmes and jolly old Dr Watson!'

Goldin clapped his plump little hands and made a magnificent gesture. At this, Milly and Dolly removed the cloth and Holmes and I stood there, revealed. There were gasps of astonishment and surprise which would have made applause something of an anti-climax. Holmes and I were known at least passingly to most of the company, including the King, who owed his very coronation to my friend. He was the first to jump up from his seat and shake us by the hands.

He said, 'Well, I don't know how young Goldin did that. I mean changing the two Arabs into a couple of English celebrities. But I don't want to enquire too closely or he might not come here to amuse us again, what! These magician fellows guard their secrets closely, I know that.'

Through the years of my association with Sherlock Holmes I have been lucky indeed to have been able to meet many people of high rank. Usually they seemed to be of a high degree of intelligence and I had assumed this to be especially true of the King. Yet he professed to be puzzled by a deception so simple that it was almost non-existent. I thought at first that he was being jocular in expressing amazement but I am a fair judge of character and I could see that he was genuine in his surprise. Goldin and I exchanged a fleeting glance which showed me that the magician was thinking very much the same thing.

However, once his astonishment had subsided a little, the King came straight to the point. 'I say, look here, Holmes. I have no idea how you got here or why, but I must tell you that on the occasion of Mr Goldin's last performance for us here a very valuable and historically important painting was found to be missing from the music-room where it had hung for many years. Please let me assure you that no suspicion ever fell upon Mr Goldin or his people who so kindly entertained us, and my guests and staff I considered all to be above suspicion. I called upon young Lestrade and he insisted that despite my lack of suspicion all of the artistes' baggage should be examined before they left, and this was done, though I hoped that they would never hear of this. But dash it, I have to mention it now because I hope you will investigate the matter. I seems that a copy of the painting had been substituted for the original which quite by chance was very quickly detected. But that did not help us to find my Rembrandt, and Lestrade has been on its trail ever since. I felt uncomfortable that Goldin might think that I might suspect him. For this reason I invited him back, also the French lady whom I feel sure is beyond any suspicion. But I did this as much that I wanted to witness their performances again and wanted my cousin Willy to share in my enjoyment this time. The sudden appearance of you and the doctor is a great surprise, a pleasant one and, dare I hope, a fortunate coincidence. After all, if you can't find my painting no one can, what? So please, Holmes, my dear fellow, can you help . . . dash it, can't imagine why I didn't think of asking you before!'

It had been a long speech, even for a king, but Holmes had shown patience unusual for him, and replied with great politeness and one could, I think, say charm.

'Your Majesty, I share your belief in the completely blameless nature of Mr Horace Goldin. Indeed, this will become clear as I expound. Although you were unaware of my presence I have been investigating the theft of your Rembrandt for several days. I will not try Your Majesty's patience with minor details, but enough to say that I decided that the exchange for the copy was made in the music-room probably whilst Mr Goldin was actually performing. The thief cut the genuine painting from its frame and substituted a very clever copy which this individual had introduced into Sandringham House in a rolled form. The genuine painting was then similarly rolled up and concealed in the same fashion.'

At this point the King interrupted. 'But dash it, Holmes, how did the blighter smuggle the thing out of the house?'

'All shall be revealed, Your Majesty, as Goldin would say, so please bear with me.'

'By Jove! Yes, rather. Please carry on, Holmes!'

During these speeches, by my friend and his King I had been watching the spectators closely. I had seen their expressions change from sheer astonishment to rapt interest and attention. Our dear Queen remained impassive, as she usually did, and the Kaiserine was likewise seemingly unmoved; but the others, including the Kaiser himself, were animated in their manner. During Holmes's words I noticed the Kaiser glance round for his aide, a very statuesque man in German army uniform, who leant over as his monarch whispered in his ear. Then the aide retreated to pass some word to his fellow, or so it seemed to me.

However, let me return the reader to Holmes's narrative . . .

'Your Majesty, because something is missing, it is not written in stone that it has been removed from the area. It is possible for something to be out of sight, yet still within a few hundred yards of its normal site.'

'You mean . . . hidden rather than stolen?'

'I mean hidden . . . prior to being actually stolen, Your Majesty.'

'Do you think you can find it for me?'

Holmes played out his words like a star actor delivering lines of great importance to the piece in which he is appearing. At the risk of boring my readers I must repeat that I am of the opinion that the London stage was robbed of a great actor when Holmes decided to become an investigator.

'Find it, sir? I think that might be arranged . . .'

I stole another peep at the audience and saw that they were now on the very edges of their seats and their nerves. The two German aides to the Kaiser stood at the back, beside the open fire which had been lit against the unseasonal chill.

Holmes continued, 'In fact, I think that Mr Goldin should make it reappear, an art at which he excels!'

Goldin walked onto the scene holding an innocent-looking cloth which he showed back and front. Then he draped it over one of his arms and with his free hand withdrew an umbrella . . . *the* umbrella . . . which he held up with an air of triumph.

He spoke with triumph in his voice as well. 'Regardez!'

Why, I ask myself, do conjurers always use that word when they wish their audience to look at something? Goldin, despite his originality in most other matters, was no exception. He was not French, yet from habit he stood there holding the umbrella and saying 'Regardez'. No wonder his greatest fame has been as a silent illusionist.

The King sat and looked at the brandished umbrella with wonderment in his gaze, as if he believed that Horace Goldin had taken leave of his senses.

'Mr Goldin, why on earth are you waving that umbrella and yelling in French? I fail to see the connection with my missing Rembrandt.'

Holmes smiled like a demon king in a pantomime. It was he who replied.

'I mentioned that the painting was rolled up, but I failed to add that it was disguised in its rolled state as an umbrella!' He pulled down the elastic top and exposed a portion of the canvas. The King was fascinated at what he was shown.

'That is my Rembrandt, rolled up and hidden in an umbrella. Why bless my soul. But who hid it there and where did you find it?'

'Where I found it, or rather where Dr Watson found it, is relatively unimportant. The main thing is that the thief, who had brought in the copy in this same adapted umbrella, made the exchange but did not take the umbrella from the premises, preferring to hide it in these precincts until a more politic time came to do so.'

'You mean, then, that whoever brought in that umbrella is the culprit?'

'I believe the owner of this umbrella has some questions to answer.'

Lestrade had sat through all of this action and dialogue like some graven image. Suddenly, however, he seemed to feel that it was time for him to play his part.

He spoke with an officious tone.

'Mr Holmes, I must remind you that the matter of the missing Rembrandt is officially mine. If you have been fortunate enough to stumble upon its place of concealment you must give it to me to keep as evidence, along with any information that you may have accumulated.'

Holmes bowed with grace and style as he took up the umbrella and handed it to the inspector. He also gave a glance to King Edward, as if to say 'We are in the hands of officialdom, what can we do?'

But in fact he said, 'Inspector, I feel sure that I have the permission of His Majesty to place this article into your hands for examination and safe keeping. Rely upon my co-operation regarding all evidence and information being made available to you. I am but a private citizen, a subject of His Majesty: my only wishes are to serve my King and country; oh, and of course to help you with your enquiries. I feel sure I need not tell you to guard the object and its hidden painting with your life.'

Lestrade took the umbrella and handed it to his sergeant who made for the entrance door to the room. Lestrade was very much on his dignity.

'You are right, you need not tell me such elementary points regarding my duties. Reynolds will take the umbrella into very safe keeping.'

As the policeman spoke, the King caught our glances and sighed, taking a gold cigarette case from his pocket. He offered the case to us as if he were dealing with barons or earls.

'I am in need of my Lady Nicotine; how about you chaps? Egyptian on one side, Virginia the other.'

As a servant hovered and lit our cigarettes I noticed that there was a minor disturbance occurring near the fireplace. Madame Francis was wrestling with the plain-clothes man to regain what was evidently her umbrella.

'Give me that, it is my parapluie!'

The policeman wrestled with her but she grabbed it with surprising agility and started for the entrance door.

Lestrade shouted after her.

'Stop, madam, in the name of the law. That umbrella may be yours, but it is evidence and you have much to answer for concerning this matter!'

King Edward was also on his feet, turning and clicking his fingers in signal to the two footmen who stood by the entrance to bar it to Madame Francis. She, realizing that she was trapped, played the only card which she felt evidently worth playing. She threw the umbrella upon the fire, where the flames quickly took a hold, and it was obvious that, despite attempts to save it, the wonderful Rembrandt painting was destroyed. She laughed as the sergeant grasped her and the footmen also held her, making escape impossible.

She shouted, 'You will be forced to release me. I have nothing to answer to. Your evidence, so called, is destroyed.'

Holmes wagged a skeletal finger in her direction.

'Madame Francis, I had suspected you since very early on in this matter. You are an artist, and a very fine one; it was you who painted the copy, and it was you who cut the original from its frame and made the substitution. You were there in the music-room alone during the very period when this must have occurred. I have searched your art materials which you use in your performance and discovered a palette knife, the tip end of its blade sharpened to razor keenness. This was doubtless used to cut the canvas from its frame. The exchange was made, but you decided not to take the umbrella with you for fear of discovery. Instead, you placed it in a crypt which you knew was never, if ever, visited and was hidden by the undergrowth.'

The King said, 'By Jove! Who would have thought it . . . dashed fine woman, too. Pity. But what the dickens did she intend to do with it, Inspector, for she could hardly have sold the confounded thing.'

He was taking the loss of his Rembrandt extremely well, seeming far more concerned with other details.

Lestrade clearly was at a loss and I nudged Holmes who,

after quite a long pause, said, 'The Inspector has already pointed out to me my lack of official involvement. But may I just opine that the painting was destined for sale to a collector who was fully aware that he could never show the painting to anyone. It would probably be hung in the cellar of some castle, entirely for its illicit owner's enjoyment, along with other lost treasures from all over the world.'

The King started. 'Good heavens, Holmes! Are there people like that?'

'Only too many of them, Your Majesty, as the Inspector will confirm. I'll wager that whoever this painting was destined for could clear up several of Scotland Yard's unsolved art theft cases. Dame Rumour is a lying jade, but has it that one extremely august European monarch has such tastes and such a cellar at one of his several castles.'

Holmes discarded the Egyptian cigarette and pleaded with his eyes to the monarch as he held up his pipe and pouch. The King nodded in understanding and the detective lit a pipeful of the Scottish mixture with a vesta before he spoke again.

'I am not in a position to make accusations, but I believe that the new owner was to take the painting home with him at the end of this delightful social visit.'

One way and another, short of using names or making direct accusation, Holmes made it clear what he meant: that the Kaiser would have had his aides collect the umbrella from the crypt before the German party left. Kaiser Wilhelm jumped to his feet and of course he not only made passionate denial, but made it clear that Holmes had hit the bull's eye.

King Edward was the picture of dignity. He did not rant or rave, indeed he spoke very quietly.

'Willy, had I known you coveted my Rembrandt I would have given it to you. Mind you, knowing your ways I imagine that would have spoiled the game, what? When I invited you to see young Goldin and you particularly requested Madame Francis also I thought nothing was strange about it; after all, as I have said, darn fine-looking woman. I am disappointed in you, Willy, and I trust you will arrange for the departure of yourself and your party forthwith.'

The Kaiser was as white as a sheet, but he nodded woodenly and rose from his chair and made from the room.

Lestrade grunted and said, 'I would have liked to have had the pleasure of arresting him, Your Majesty, and I would have had he not been a relative of yours.'

The King smiled bitterly and said, 'Come, Inspector, we don't want a jolly old international incident. It's my loss, but then I never used to look at the wretched painting anyway.'

Holmes leapt in with a bombshell of a remark. 'In that case, Your Majesty would not appreciate it if Mr Goldin could work even more of his magic and restore your painting to you?'

'Come, Holmes, you mock me. Not done, old chap, mocking one's monarch!' The King was still surprisingly affable.

It was Goldin who broke in at this point.

'If Your Majesty would allow it I will do my best to do as Mr Holmes suggests. Please to follow me . . .'

The magician walked with as much dignity as his build would allow and beckoned us to follow him as he made for the music-room. The King seemed a little bewildered as he did as he was bade, but after all it was but a few paces.

Inside the music-room, Goldin pointed to the hanging

frame with a little black stick with its white ends which he called his magic wand.

'Your Majesty, Mrs Queen, ladies and gentlemen. Behold that which the flames destroyed is now magically restored!'

I confess I began to think that Goldin and Holmes had gone clean off their heads until I studied the signature on the painting. Even I, with the recent experience of studying both examples, was able to pronounce that this was indeed the original Rembrandt, and said as much.

'It is indeed the portrait that was stolen, Your Majesty. That which was lost is now indeed found, without a shadow of a doubt.'

It was Lestrade who spoke first after myself. 'You mean the French woman somehow learned of your plans, Holmes, and switched the paintings back again?'

But Holmes chuckled as he clarified the point. 'No, that would hardly have been to her advantage as it transpired. No, it was I who made the substitution, fearing some last-minute risk of its loss. So now, given that the painting is properly guarded from this moment, all is indeed well that ends well.'

I wish, dear reader, that I could say that this was the end of the story. But few real-life dramas conclude at the point where a playwright would wish them to.

CHAPTER FOUR

The Vanishing Detective

King Edward was truly delighted to not only regain his priceless Rembrandt but also to find that he had Sherlock Holmes as a house guest as well as his favourite magician Horace Goldin. The King, it can now be told, many years after his sad demise, was very fond of music-hall and vaudeville-type entertainments. When he was Prince of Wales he had haunted the stage doors of the leading London variety theatres, but where the noble lords usually courted the chorus girls. Many a 'lady' had graced the chorus of the Gaiety at one time; His Majesty had reached for the 'stars' with Miss Langtry, the famous 'Jersey Lilly' being a prominent example of his taste in lovely women. However, an interest in magicians and illusionists, although genuine in his case, had given him the perfect excuse to visit the stage doors. Madame Francis had been one of the King's most recent 'discoveries', but she had turned out to be a very unwise choice for a royal friendship. However, he seemed strangely unperturbed at her arrest and, for that matter, the rift with his Germanic cousin which had resulted from the Rembrandt affair.

As we sat over our port, the ladies having withdrawn after that night's splendid dinner, the King confided, 'You know, gentlemen, this tiff with the Kaiser was inevitable, really. It would have arisen over Holland, Belgium, France or some such other place in Europe sooner or later. Between ourselves, I think he would have taken a crack at us before this is he was not related to me. He wants our colonies, you know. But don't worry; if it came to war we would soon show him what's what, what?'

We all laughed politely, but Holmes appeared a little tense upon the subject.

He said, gently, 'Your Majesty will forgive me if I utter a word of advice. I have travelled extensively upon the Continent, and I can assure you that the Kaiser is preparing to conquer France, Belgium, aye and whisper it, even ourselves. He has many weapons of offence that we do not seem to possess. Airships, capable of dropping explosives onto our cities, for example.'

The King chuckled as he made light of it.

'My dear chap, forgive me, but I think you have been reading far too many stories by Jules Verne and H G Wells. Britannia rules the waves and don't you forget it. As it is cousin Willy and his party are already on the jolly old briny as I speak. Let's talk about something else.'

This was Goldin's cue to make some salt disappear from his cupped hand, swallow a table knife and bend the King's watch without damaging it. One way and another Goldin had given the King a feast of magic during his short stay. But I sensed that Holmes was a little distracted.

He whispered to me, 'I shall take a stroll in the grounds, Watson. Pray give my apologies to the King, Mr Goldin and the others, if they miss me.'

As it happened, Sherlock Holmes was not missed for quite a few minutes, and then my excuse that he had been feeling a little faint and needed fresh air was accepted easily enough.

The King said, 'The good fellow has had enough activity to make anyone faint, what?'

I secretly thought that he had perhaps wanted to take one last look to see that the painting was safe, and as soon as I was decently able to get away I made for the music-room, but the fact that my entrance to that apartment was barred by a burly manservant showed that he would have had no worry on that score. I took a turn in the grounds but did not find Holmes out on the terrace, smoking his pipe as I had half expected to. He was not in the splendid new quarters that had been made available to us, so I returned to the party, where the gentlemen had by now joined the ladies.

The indefatigable Goldin was showing card tricks, and he continued to do so until most of us were ready to go up the wooden hill to Bedfordshire. But of course it was polite to await a yawn or two from the King before making any suggestion of retiring.

Then, at about midnight, the King intimated that those who wished to retire were welcome to do so.

'My dear friends, pray do not wait for me to make the first move in the direction of bed. It is my habit to play a few hands of cards before retiring.'

Gratefully, most of them left for their beds, but Goldin and I were more or less press-ganged into the card session. I don't think Goldin needed much enticement; in fact, I don't believe that Goldin ever sleeps!

I have to say that for a superb card manipulator Mr

Goldin is an extremely poor poker player. I thought at first that he was deliberately allowing the King to win for diplomatic reasons, but during a break in the play I confronted him with the question and he said, 'Doc, just because I can produce the four aces any time I want during a performance does not help me to play cards. I am just not good at poker, although I love to play.'

Later Milly and Dolly would confirm this. 'The guv'nor only hires assistants who play poker, always believing that he can win back the wages he has paid them, but he always loses!'

Having lost what little money I had to His Majesty, I beg-ged to be allowed to retire and he let me go with good grace.

'By Jove, Watson, I owe you much. It's a bit thick to take your money, but that is poker, what?'

I retired to my room which was next to Holmes's apartment, and I decided to take a quick look to see if he was asleep. His door was slightly ajar, so this was not difficult, or rather would not have been had my friend been present. But he was not. I found this perhaps less surprising than one might think, knowing the erratic habits of my friend so well. I felt that he had doubtless decided to stroll in the grounds, and I admired his constitution being such as to enable him to.

On the morrow I looked into his room on my way to breakfast. He was not there but I was still not greatly surprised because he is inclined to rise earlier than I. But a glance round the room did make me a little intrigued with the fact that despite our imminent departure he had made no attempt whatever to begin to pack his things.

When I found that he was not at the breakfast table I

began to feel a little bit concerned. Goldin was there, shovelling away vast quantities of sausage, bacon, mushrooms and fried bread. As he finished, the butler asked him if he wanted sugar with his coffee but he waved a podgy hand and said, 'No, my friend, I got to watch my waistline!'

I asked Horace, Milly, Dolly and all other relevant persons if they had seen anything of Holmes.

None of them had so I asked the butler, who said, 'The last I saw of Mr Holmes, sir, was last night, after he had left the drawing-room, and was being helped by two other gentlemen, on account of being a little under the weather.'

I started at this, realizing that the butler meant to imply, judging from the way he spoke and his facial expression, that Holmes had been drinking too much. I knew that this was not true, having spent the evening in his company, an evening during which he had drunk scarcely two glasses of champagne and an after-dinner liqueur. I pressed the butler for more details.

'Who were these two gentlemen who were helping him?'

'Why, sir, they were His Majesty the Kaiser's aides.'

'What?'

'Is something wrong, sir?'

'I don't know. Where are the Kaiser's aides now?'

'Why, sir, they left earlier this morning with his Germanic Majesty and his Queen. I did think they left with a rather sudden style. But then, Doctor, rumour has it that the Kaiser had a few words with King Edward . . .' He tailed off, realizing that he was, for a servant, starting to border on the impertinent.

At this point I made a request for an audience with the King, saying that the matter was of the utmost importance. Servants scurried about, and eventually all protocol was cast aside and I was taken to the King's bedroom where he was still reclining with his breakfast upon a tray before him.

'Ah, young Watson! What can I do for you? Pull up a chair, don't stand on ceremony. Like some breakfast?'

As ever, King Edward was bluff, hearty and extremely likeable. I explained that I had breakfasted and that I was concerned for the welfare of my friend, and he immediately became seemingly as concerned as I. His huge dressing gown was brought and he arose from his bed, aided by two servants who helped him into the robe. Within a couple of minutes he was issuing orders and there was a buzz of activity. Soldiers were to search the grounds, servants were to search the house, and a wire was to be sent to Southampton where the Kaiser would board, with his party, a German royal yacht.

'If it is a case of abduction, my navy people will see to it! Meanwhile we must search everywhere, and I will send some guardsmen on horseback to follow the royal Germany party in case they can be waylaid before they reach Southampton. Oh yes, and we must alert Lestrade. He has left, don't you know, believing that all that he could do was done.'

When Lestrade arrived he was surprisingly concerned for a man who had been made to seem rather foolish only the day before. But the inspector had, I knew, an enormous respect for Holmes, as a man as well as an investigator, even if he would have been loath to voice his admiration.

He said to me, 'You and I, Doctor, will take a look round lest anything gets overlooked. By the way, I have wired London to make sure that he hasn't turned up at Baker Street.'

I thought this unlikely; Holmes, casual as he could be in

his manners, would scarcely have left for Baker Street without me. But I thanked Lestrade for thinking of it and indeed I was glad of his support.

The inspector and I made a very thorough tour of the house first, to make sure that no closet or alcove had been overlooked. Frequently Lestrade blew his police whistle, and listened for any answering reaction. Then, when we both were convinced that he could not have been imprisoned and hidden anywhere within we took to the grounds and repeated the whole process, complete with frequent blasts upon the whistle. But the grounds, of course, were very extensive and I realized that we would need to leave much of this work to the soldiers who were fanning out like so many beaters at a grouse shoot.

Later that day we consulted again with the King who was more than helpful. Goldin needed to go to the theatre and was sent off in the direction of London in a Royal Daimler, assuring me that he would keep in close touch. I asked His Majesty if the cavalry had as yet caught up with the German party.

He nodded. 'They are being held at Winchester. I had wired the police at several towns through which they would pass before that, but they all wired back with little or nothing to report.' He chuckled as he continued, 'Old Willy must be sick of his party being held up.'

I enquired, 'Is it possible that he sent Holmes by a different route to his own and is holding him on the yacht?'

The King shook his head. 'Not unless he had a couple of other aides hidden up somewhere. But I'll send you to Southampton so that you can satisfy yourself that he is not on the yacht. My own personal motor-car will be ready to take you in ten minutes.'

Lestrade went with me in the Rolls-Royce motor-car, which took us to Southampton in a truly astonishingly short time. I doubt if an express train would have done much better, even assuming that such a vehicle should have been scheduled for a direct journey. As it happened, we beat the German party to Southampton in their horse-drawn carriage.

The yacht had already been well searched by the local naval authorities but we still went through the motions of a search. The Kaiser and his Queen, the Kaiserine, were furious by this time but could scarcely avoid collaboration. Already they were bearing the disgrace of the obvious slur of the attempt to steal the Rembrandt portrait. When Lestrade and I confronted the Kaiser I was struck with how very obese he was, a fact which emphasized the shortness of his deformed left arm.

He glowered at us. 'Inspector, Herr Doctor, I am insulted by your attentions and insinuations. It is bad enough to be accused, wrongly yes, of attempting to steal your King's Rembrandt, but for you to suggest that I would attempt to abduct your stupid detective. What possible advantage to me, huh!'

I saw no point in angering him further, simply saying, 'Your Majesty, we must pursue all avenues in order to find what has happened to Sherlock Holmes.'

It is said that the soft answer turneth away wrath and this seemed true in the case of the Kaiser.

'Well, Herr Doctor, I have no quarrel with you: I only hope that the bad feeling that all this business will produce between our two countries will not affect you as much as it certainly will others . . . My foolish cousin will pay . . . he will pay . . .'

I jumped to my feet. 'You speak, sir, of my King. I cannot allow you to speak of him like that!'

'Enough, the audience is over!'

We were told in no uncertain tones that our room would be preferred to our company and we left the yacht which had been searched very thoroughly by now. Lestrade and I climbed into the royal car for the return journey, but stopped for the night at a coaching inn near Hertford. We agreed, Lestrade and I, that we could do little more to immediately help the situation. In fact, we even took the step of sending the royal car back to Sandringham as we could easily get an early train back to London, from where we could possibly do more.

The landlord of the White Hart was a jovial fellow as innkeepers so often are, and he produced for us a splendid mutton pie, despite the lateness of the hour.

As he served us, he said, 'I must have known deep down that a couple of real gents like yourselves would be a stopping off. I had some fellows early in the day demanding a meat pie for their master who they said would not leave his coach. Some sort of foreign nobleman he must have been, but I sent out some beer and sausages, bread, cheese and pickles. Good enough for anyone who will not even bother to enter my premises.'

He had my attention now. 'How many people altogether?'

'Well now, let me see, there was the lord and his lady, if that's what they were, that's two; a maid makes three; coach driver and postilion, that's five; and these two great brutes of servants. Seven of 'em altogether.'

Lestrade and I exchanged a glance.

Then Lestrade asked, 'Did they give any idea where they

were bound, landlord?'

'Oh aye, sir, Southampton. They was using the best road.'

We discussed what the good host had said as he wandered off to fetch another jug of his excellent home brew.

'What do you make of that, Lestrade? He obviously spoke of the Kaiser's party.'

'He did, sir, and this was not one of the places where we had them observed. You never know, we might find out something here. Now what would Mr Holmes do next if he was here?'

'He would certainly question the other members of the inn staff.'

'That he would, let's start with the barmaid.'

We left our table to sit upon the saddle stools at the bar counter. When the comely lady served us we tried to be casual in our introduction of the subject of the Germans.

'Very arrogant they were, sir, and rather scruffy when they first arrived. They went off to the bathroom to wash and brush up and when they returned they looked much better. I had to clean that room after them, and the floor was smothered in leaves and stuff that they had brushed off their jackets.'

Lestrade and I exchanged glances and he raised an eyebrow. When the barmaid was busy at the other end of the bar, he remarked, 'Curious, Doctor. I mean that the Kaiser's aides should have arrived here in a scruffy state. What could have made them so, for I feel sure that they would have been immaculate when they left Sandringham.'

'Indeed, yet I cannot picture any incident which could have happened upon their journey to this point that could have caused them to be covered in leaves.'

'The bathroom floor has been cleaned, but possibly there may be a brush in the bathroom that still has tell-tale traces of flora!'

We decided to visit the washroom in turn rather than together, and then to compare notes afterwards. I felt that this would seem rather more normal and cause no surprise among those at the inn. It was my turn to make the first such excursion and I casually arose, saying that I must wash my hands.

The apartment was empty and I crossed eagerly to the row of wash taps and sinks. There was a mirror and a shelf beneath it bearing various clothes brushes. I examined one of these closely and found some traces of vegetation, though fine and sparse, but on the second brush I had more success. I shook some scraps of vegetation onto an envelope which I took from my pocket and tipped it into another. The floor was clean, as I had expected. I could find nothing else of interest so I quickly returned to the bar.

Lestrade looked up at me with a quizzical expression. I nodded as if to say 'I found something', and he arose to walk towards the bathroom.

When he had gone the barmaid said, 'Very tall, your friend, but he could do with brightening up his dress a bit. Those dark clothes and hat make him look too much like a policeman.'

When the inspector returned he shrugged to indicate that he had found nothing of note, but later when we were alone he showed me a similar grain or two of foliage in an envelope to that which rested in my wallet.

'What do you make of it, Doctor?'

'It appears to be mostly some kind of dried moss, like

tiny living particles. Other than that there are a few grassheads and the like which they could have picked up anywhere.'

The following morning we took the train to Victoria and from thence a cab to Baker Street. I suppose there was not much at 221B that would tell Lestrade anything but he insisted on going there with me.

We paced the sitting-room, handling the pipes and albums, as if this would bring back the great detective himself. Mrs Hudson fussed around, distraught that anything should have happened to her famous lodger.

'To think, Doctor, that only a few days ago I was tellin' him off for making the place untidy. If he was here now he could do whatever he liked, so he could. You know, Dr Watson, it is not until you lose somebody that you think of all the good things about them. Then you start to think of all your own shortcomings. Recently I have done nothing but pester poor Mr Holmes about losing my property to these Crown people! It doesn't seem like a problem any more, compared with what has happened!'

Despite his preoccupation with Holmes's mysterious disappearance, Lestrade was sympathetic concerning the fate of 221B.

'Doesn't seem right; why, this place is like an institution; and I don't mean a hospital or an asylum. I just can't imagine Mr Holmes or yourself, or for that matter dear Mrs Hudson, anywhere else.'

The good lady touched an eye with her handkerchief and busied herself, saying that she would fetch us a pot of coffee from the kitchen.

As soon as she had left the room, Lestrade spoke upon

the subject again. 'Will the old girl get another place where she can let rooms do you think, Doctor?'

I answered, 'Well, she must get some kind of compensation, but it has always been my experience that such payments are never enough to replace that which has been taken.'

'What does Holmes think about it?'

'It's difficult to say. The subject conflicted with the problem that Goldin brought to him. You know how single-minded he can be, though I feel sure he will give Mrs Hudson's troubles his undivided attention when . . . when he gets back . . .' I tailed off, stopping myself from adding '*if* he gets back', which was in my mind.

I took the envelope from my wallet and carefully dropped the moss onto a sheet of white paper. I looked at it for a few minutes with the aid of one of Holmes's lenses and searched for inspiration.

Then, in agony of mind, I turned to Lestrade and said, 'All of these years I have assisted Sherlock Holmes with his investigations and even vied with him at times to produce deductions. One would think that I would have learned his methods to the extent that I could find some clue at the very time when he most needs me to!'

Lestrade nodded sadly and expressed a similar view. 'I never admitted it to him, but I have always realized that he was my superior when it came to the scientific aspect of crime detection. Holmes and I made a good team, really, because I had the patience to indulge in all the down-to-earth aspects. What you might call the foot-slogging of detective work. Holmes supplied the inspiration and I supplied the perspiration. As for you, Doctor, you were always a ray of sanity and of course a great diplomat. Many has been the time when if Holmes and I had been left to work without your mediation we would have quarrelled, which is something we never did, thanks to a great extent to yourself.'

At this point Mrs Hudson bustled in with a pot of hot coffee on a tray with two cups, a milk jug and sugar bowl. She placed this down upon the table, making it necessary to move my sheet of paper bearing its granules of foliage.

She looked at it with distaste. 'Goodness, Doctor, what have you got there? You surely didn't brush up that dust in here? I've been all over this room only this morning with a duster and a dustpan and brush. But I was at the cemetery last night to put flowers on my sister's grave, it having been her birthday, poor soul, and maybe some of it got on my skirt.'

I was puzzled by her meaning for a few seconds, but very soon the full meaning of her words became clear.

I enquired, 'Mrs Hudson, am I to understand that there was some dust like this at the cemetery?'

She replied sharply, 'Well, of course, Doctor. That's the stuff that gathers on gravestones. I suppose it's a sort of moss, but it dries up and comes off if you touch it. But I didn't think there was any left on me when I came in this room.'

Lestrade leapt in with a question to the good lady.

'Mrs Hudson, let us get this quite clear; you mean that the dust on that paper reminds you of that which brushes off gravestones?'

'Why yes, Inspector. There's lots of stuff just like that at the cemetery.'

Lestrade and I both gasped, and our eyes met with the identical thought which the good lady's words inspired.

There was no need for either of us to **state the** obvious; that Mrs Hudson's words had made us both think in terms of Holmes having been taken to a graveyard, either alive and imprisoned or dead and to be concealed. I suppose I spoke first, as memory serves.

'Lestrade, is there any sort of a graveyard near Sandringham House?'

'There are several, at various villages and hamlets with churches and cemeteries.'

'We must search them all!'

'I am afraid you are right!'

And so it was that we left Baker Street almost as soon as we had returned. I told Mrs Hudson that we were off to Sandringham again, but I tried to cheer the poor tearful lady as best I could.

'Mrs Hudson, be cheered by the fact that we have now at least some kind of a clue as to what might have happened to Mr Holmes. If we do find him, as I hope we will, it will be *your* remark about the gravestone moss that will have put us onto the trail.'

CHAPTER FIVE

To Find Sherlock Holmes

We took the train to King's Lynn, Lestrade and I, but please, dear reader, ask me for no descriptions of rolling countryside, lakes, rivers or nice little white-painted cottages because I was fast asleep within five minutes of the train making its first movement. But when I awoke as we pulled into King's Lynn the tall Scotland Yard man was wide awake and I have his word that he had remained so throughout the journey.

Indeed, Lestrade had been working hard with maps and notebooks making a list of burial places which it would have been practical for the two Germans to have taken our friend during the time available to them. We made first for the tearoom where I drank hot black coffee and listened to his extremely meticulous reading from the notes that he had made.

'Doctor, we have to remember that they had several hours during which to do whatever they did with Holmes, assuming that he was abducted at around midnight, as seems likely. I reckon that they could have taken him to any of all but a dozen places of burial that I have listed; all within ten miles of Sandringham House.'

'You consider they might have taken him so far? Perhaps to begin with we should confine ourselves to places within five miles of the Royal residence.'

He agreed that this was sensible. I was amazed at how calm he had remained, with my own nerves being by this stage at breaking point.

We spent the rest of that day with a hired gig, making a tour of graveyards, church premises and cemeteries. We were looking, as we weaved between the tombstones, for some sign of a stone that had recently had its mosses disturbed. We also inspected the interiors of churches and cemetery buildings for the possibility of concealment of a body or prisoner. As night fell we were no nearer to finding Sherlock Holmes than before we started our journey from London.

We put up for the night in a local police cottage, where Lestrade's credentials were enough to get us a good meal and a comfortable bed. Sergeant Murdoch and his wife Georgina treated us like royalty. Her steak and kidney pie was a wonder, which I would have enjoyed the more had Holmes been there to share it. As it was I could scarcely manage more than two helpings.

Sergeant George Murdoch was a jolly enough man, though I sensed that just below his veneer of rustic good nature was a mind that was deeper than his rank and situation would have suggested. He was a little in awe of Lestrade, of course, but with me he chatted easily and explained that he and his wife were great enthusiasts for my accounts of my friend's adventures.

'The missus and I are both Georges, so I and our friends call her Gina. We thought that *The Hound of the Baskervilles* was the most exciting of all the adventures. Gina wept when you told us in *The Final Problem* of the untimely death of your friend. Then, when he turned up again, we had a celebration meal: pray God that we will be having another one sometime in the next few days.'

As Georgina Murdoch cleared our plates and brought us steaming hot mugs of coffee I decided that there could be no harm in laying all the facts before these bright, honest people, beyond the broad story that we had already given them, lest their local knowledge might make this fruitful. I noticed that Lestrade was a little uncomfortable as I told them the story. To him a local sergeant was not necessarily a person to be taken completely into one's confidence, rather just someone to issue orders to. However, I followed my instinct.

The inspector was later to admit that my opening out to them was a wise move. After I had filled in most of the details, George Murdoch leaned forward in his chair, his honest ruddy face betraying a certain suppressed excitement as he enquired, 'Inspector Lestrade, might I be allowed to enquire if either of you has a sample of this moss that you mention?'

'I believe Dr Watson has a grain or two in his wallet, but what makes you ask that, Sergeant?'

'Well sir, my missus, Gina, is a bit of an expert on such things, in a very small way, of course. But she has a small conservatory in the back garden, and grows all sorts of creepers and wild plants.'

I leapt in lest Lestrade should let his rank spoil an outside chance of some kind of help being given us. I was desperate for the life of a dear friend and protocol no longer interested me!'

'Mrs Murdoch, Georgina, if you would look at this sample I would be more than grateful.'

I took the envelope from my wallet and poured some grains onto a visiting card for her inspection. The good lady reached for her spectacles. She peered through them at my pathetic little heap of dust with interest. She then pronounced upon them.

'I don't know the Latin name for it, Dr Watson, but what you have there is a few dried fragments of a sort of fungi that abounds on stone, especially old stone.'

'My landlady said as much, opining that it might have come off a gravestone in a churchyard or cemetery.'

'There are several kinds, sir, and all rather similar. But this particular kind usually grows on old stones that are fairly dry. I have, for instance, an old sundial in my conservatory and since I placed it there that particular growth has attacked it. I will show you if you like.'

Lestrade had lost all his doubts now and we both jumped at her offer. She took us out into the modest back garden and into a small conservatory. This was unusual in the type of plants and objects within. There were cacti and dry creepers, and the centrepiece was indeed a very mature sundial. Sure enough, upon it there was a good deal of the mossy growth we had grown so involved with.

She explained, 'You see, sir, it gets very little water save what might be spilled around it from my can. The rain does not touch it in here so this dry form of the weed has all but covered parts of it. I do not remove it because I think it gives a rather, how shall I say, a mature appearance.'

Sergeant Murdoch was almost apologetic concerning his wife's refinement. 'Begging your pardon, gentlemen, but my wife, you see, was a lady's maid in one of the big houses. There her lady grew very fond of her and imparted all manner of education that she would hardly have learned at the dame's school that she attended until she was twelve.'

I could not resist my reply. 'Sergeant Murdoch, you do not need to apologize for the knowledge that your wife has acquired. Remember, there has to be a lively mind present before any learning can be absorbed.'

Then I spoke to his wife. 'You have been more than helpful, Mrs Murdoch, and you could well have narrowed our search to a very important extent.'

Even Lestrade gave grudging praise. 'Your wife is a credit to you, Sergeant, and I believe we are making progress at last.'

It was Sergeant George Murdoch's turn to try and assist us.

'If I might be so bold, Inspector, may I express the view that you should be searching the grounds at Sandringham House for some hidden nook or cranny.'

But Lestrade was a little dismissive of this opinion. 'The police and about two dozen soldiers have searched the grounds with a fine-toothed comb and found no clue!'

The sergeant persisted. 'But Inspector, you and the others were not quite sure what signs to look for at that time and might have overlooked something which you would be searching for in light of the knowledge gained since then.'

Lestrade nodded grudgingly. 'There may be something in what you say. Watson; we will return to Sandringham early tomorrow. It could do no harm for us to give the grounds another look.'

I agreed, feeling that this would make better sense than widening our search; especially since we had gained the important clue from Mrs Murdoch which would make us less interested in open graveyards.

That night I tried to sleep but slept only in short snatches, with nightmares waking me at regular intervals. These horrific dreams featured Sherlock Holmes, buried alive, cast into a pond in a weighted shroud, thrown from the battlements of Sandringham House onto a multitude of bayonets and bricked up in a basement wall. Every time, when I found him in these dreams, he muttered, 'Alas, you have arrived too late. You know my methods, what kept you so long?' Then he would expire and I would awaken in a feverish frenzy.

Despite my restless night I managed a good breakfast and suggested to Lestrade that we should take Sergeant Murdoch with us. He was a little doubtful but eventually agreed when Murdoch assured us that his wife was capable of holding the fort, as he expressed it.

'There is little crime in this area; it is more a case of her taking messages for matters that are not very urgent.'

Taking him with us did, of course, solve any transport problem, for Murdoch had a police gig and a splendid if rather corpulent bay gelding. It was no more than thirty minutes after leaving the police cottage before we saw the gates of Sandringham House ahead of us.

The gatekeeper was very surprised to see us and I doubt if we would have gained entrance without the presence of Inspector Lestrade. As it was, there was a certain grudging manner among the staff. I believe that the gardeners and outdoor staff had the feeling that they had suffered enough disturbance since the disappearance of Sherlock Holmes. But inside, the atmosphere was different and we were assured that even the King himself would be anxious to speak with us.

King Edward was indeed a very democratic monarch. I had always heard that this was so, but I was now to have a personal experience of his casual style. We were ushered into a side-room and given coffee, assured that His Majesty would be down to see us within a short while. Yes and indeed within ten minutes His Majesty entered, in his dressing gown and unattended by servants or ministers.

He greeted us warmly and made a sincere enquiry regarding the progress we had made in finding Sherlock Holmes.

'You know, Inspector, Doctor, Sergeant, I have the greatest possible personal regard for Sherlock Holmes. Just before my coronation the bally Crown Jewels were suddenly missing. I don't need to tell you, Watson, and I am sure you remember, Lestrade, that it was Holmes who was responsible for their recovery, aided by Sir William Gillette, the actor, of all people. So I owe my coronation, my very crown to Sherlock Holmes. Afterwards he would take no reward, not even a knighthood! What can I do for you, gentlemen? I will do whatever I can to help in your search.'

We declined an offer of a crowd of soldiers and gardeners, feeling that the use of these people before might have been a mistake. All we asked was permission to go where we wished in the grounds and this the King most gladly granted.

'I see what you mean, gentlemen; three men who know exactly what they are looking for, stand a better chance unencumbered by others. Too many cooks rather ruin the jolly old soup, what?'

The King was a bit vague with his quotation but we knew what he meant and agreed that he had hit the nail on the head. We departed for the Sandringham grounds with the blessing of our monarch, and, I was heartened to feel, the goodwill of all who had ever read any of my accounts of the adventures of Sherlock Holmes.

We spent many hours fanning out, searching and reconvening to discuss what we had seen. We all paid particular attention to greenhouses, conservatories, summer houses and any sort of half-forgotten shelter, of which there were many.

Returning to the house to meet and compare notes at about four of the clock we were served with tea.

'Lestrade, I cannot think that we have missed anything that the earlier searchers would not have stumbled upon. Mind you, there are always half-forgotten nooks and crannies in grounds as extensive as these. I mean, look how I stumbled upon that crypt where we found the stolen painting. I imagine that was one of the first places where the official search party looked.'

'Of course, Doctor, but that would perhaps have been a bit too obvious.'

My words seemed to strike some sort of chord in the inspector's mind.

'What was it that Mr Holmes used to say? Eliminate the impossible and even the obvious may present the solution?'

'Those were not his actual words, Lestrade, but I follow the train of your thought. Perhaps there would be no harm in taking another look at the crypt.'

I gave Lestrade a rather more formal version than was in fact the true one concerning my discovery of that bizarre and well-concealed edifice. Actually it was no longer so well concealed by underbrush, through the attentions that had been given to it during the recent past. It was locked, but Lestrade dealt with that problem, using the simplest of the picks which he habitually carried.

As he manipulated the aged, simple mechanism he muttered, 'No need to trouble His Majesty or, for that matter, waste valuable time.'

There was a sharp click and a satisfied grunt as the old lock turned. The door moved with an eerie creak, and we stepped into the dark chamber. Lestrade, enterprising as ever, produced his pocket lamp which, through a magnifying lens, threw out quite a strong light.

He grinned. 'I don't usually approve of new-fangled inventions, Doctor, but I had to get one of these. Now look around and you will see that there is no place where a prisoner or a body could be concealed. There are no alcoves and the floor is solid and unchanged in possibly a century. There are just these three immovable sarcophagi and even that umbrella in which the painting was hidden could not be concealed from view in here.'

He was right, and we had to give up on the crypt and turned our attention to yet another fruitless search of the undergrowth and shrubberies.

Then we dismally returned to the house, hoping that the dawning of a new day might bring with it inspiration. The King had arranged a splendid meal for us, one that we could partake of whenever the opportunity occurred. Then, after a pipe in the gardens, we turned in, laying our heads upon satin pillows in the two splendid bedrooms that had been made available to us.

I slept for a while, fitfully, as on the previous night. Then the nightmares began, with Holmes being discovered in so many unlikely places; alive, dead or in some ghastly state that was midway between these two conditions. Then suddenly I was wide awake and sitting bolt upright in the bed.

My mind was working very clearly now and the last of the nightmares seemed to suggest the connection with the moss-dust that had momentarily slipped my mind. Now it was very much to the front of my thoughts again. I arose, slipped on a dressing gown and took up the oil lamp. (The royal residences were not as yet entirely lit by electric means.) I dashed out onto the landing and hammered upon Lestrade's door.

'Lestrade, quick, I think I have the answer, but if I am right every minute counts and it well may be already too late!'

'What, what? Pray, what is ado, Doctor? Let me at least put on my robe!'

Within half a minute he joined me, in his dressing gown, but had also got into his boots. His hair stood erect, giving him a comic appearance in the flickering light of the oil lamp.

He gasped, rather than spoke. 'Upon my word, Dr Watson, do you realize what o'clock it is . . . what on earth . . . ?'

But I was quite collected now. 'Quickly now, Lestrade, the game is afoot. We must go directly to the crypt. I will go first and leave it to you to follow with some men, gardeners or their like, with spades and levers!'

If my inspiration was right I had no time to wait longer and I fairly raced down the stairs and out of the nearest egress that I could unfasten. It took me no more than two minutes to reach the entrance to the crypt.

The reader will doubtless be familiar with the age-old expression, more haste, less speed. I should, of course, have waited to be given a key to the crypt or at least for Lestrade to join me with his lock-picking contraption. In my haste I had forgotten that detail; the fact that we had neatly refastened the lock upon leaving the crypt a few hours earlier. In my anguish I threw myself at the heavy oak door, trying to break it open as if it had been some flimsy modern counterpart. Needless to say, I made little effect upon it.

However, very soon Lestrade was at my side. 'Calm yourself, Doctor. Upon my word, I have never known you to be in such a frenzied state before. Here, I'll soon have it open.'

He had, of course, thought to bring the pick which would open the door, and with deliberate, deft movements he did so, despite my erratic holding of the lamp. Then we burst into the crypt and Lestrade looked about him as I held up the lamp. There was a very slight tinge of irony in his voice.

'Now, Dr Watson, calm down and tell me what it is that has brought us here at this ungodly hour.'

I noted that he was indeed leading a party of three or four workmen with spades, levers and axes. I suddenly realized what an exhibition I might be making of myself, especially if my inspiration was wrong. I calmed myself and tried to explain clearly.

'Lestrade, I suddenly remembered as I awoke from a nightmare that it was that mossy dust or some exactly like it that abounded in here. See how it has accumulated upon the large sarcophagus, especially around the edge of the stone lid. It suddenly came into my mind that the dust was completely covering that area when Holmes and I had examined it. Yet when you and I were here an hour or two ago there was a border to this near side where the stone was without moss, as if it had been moved during the past few days. This would account for the dust on the Germans' clothes.'

Lestrade was sceptical, as were the Sandringham gardeners. He spoke with urgency, still sensing my anxiety.

'You mean the two Germans collared Holmes, perhaps chloroformed him, opened the lid of the sarcophagus and put him inside, replacing the top? A tall story; Murphy, you have worked here a long time, would it be possible for two men to move that lid?'

The gardener scratched his head. 'Hard to say, sir. Nobody has ever tried to shift it as far as I know. But they were big burly fellows, weren't they?'

The inspector spoke that which was in my own mind. 'Come, we are wasting time. The lid has been shifted recently, even if only by an inch or so; there are five of us, let us try and move it. Watson, place the lamp on one of the other stone coffins and give us a hand.'

I did as he bade me and between us we managed to shift the stone cover enough to make the insertion of the spades and levers possible. Between us we managed to move the lid to the extent that it fell to the floor upon one side of the stone casket.

I had been aware of an unsavoury smell within the crypt before. Now, however, an indescribable stench filled the chamber. My kerchief across my mouth I dared to rise upon my toes and peer into the stone interior, fearful of what I might see.

'Good heavens, it is Holmes!' I all but shrieked the words as I clambered up the better to see what had befallen my poor dear friend. He lay there in his tail suit, his face ashen, his eyelids closed. I had not my stethoscope but I put my ear to his chest and detected some movement of his heart. He was alive, but only just!

We lifted him out of the grisly resting place which he

had occupied for so long. Taking him from the crypt we laid him upon the underbrush. The fresh night air did more than any efforts of mine might have, and very soon his facial muscles twitched and his eyes opened.

'It is a chilly night for the season, is it not, my dear Watson?'

The words were barely audible, yet told me that we had arrived just in time!

There was no time for protocol, so we carried Holmes into the house and, pushing all protesters aside, we laid him upon a beautiful regency couch in the large impressive hallway. I moistened his lips with water and a few minutes later I managed to spoon a few drops into his mouth. Later still, he demanded a glass of water and I knew that he was saved. He also requested some broth which I had the kitchen staff prepare; but I delayed feeding it to him until we had him safely in a clean bed. We had undressed and washed him as best we could, but his strength was all but spent.

He slept for three hours, then awoke, sufficiently recovered to raise himself upon his elbows and demand his pipe and tobacco. I knew that it was useless to argue with him so I myself lit the pipe and started it burning, handing him the glorious bowlful of narcotic which could scarcely harm a man who had managed to survive some fifty hours in a stone coffin with a century-old corpse!

I tried to keep Holmes from using his strength in narration, doing all the talking I could and bringing him up to date upon our adventures. He seemed patronizingly amused at my account of our adventures. Then at last he sat up in bed and nothing that I could say or do could stop him from relating what had happened to him.

'The two ruffians grabbed hold of me as soon as I left you to your social amusements, Watson. They swiftly clapped a pad of chloroform to my face. There was no one about, until we got near to the door to the gardens through which they took me. The last thing that I can remember hearing was one of the Germans speaking, perhaps to a footman. He said, "Herr Holmes has had too much to drink. We are taking him for a walk in the grounds to sober him." When I recovered my senses, we were then in the crypt, where by the light of a dark lantern they shifted the top from that dreadful sarcophagus. They were both enormously strong, but, as you can imagine from your own experience, it was amazing that they were able to shift it. I was not recovered enough to do anything to escape, simply lying in a heap in the corner of the crypt. But I had the power of speech and I said, "If you imprison me in there, sir, I will die within twelve hours. Is any painting, masterpiece or not, worth indulging in murder?" But they had no feelings; one of them was coarse in his reply. "Anyone who gets in the way of the King of Prussia must be dealt with. No one will find you, especially that fool of a doctor or that dolt from Scotland Yard. Although I suppose you may be discovered in a few hundred years from now by some archaeologist!" '

Holmes continued, 'There was space enough for me to lie upon the top of the occupant of the coffin. As they replaced the stone top I knew it was useless for me to struggle or even shout with any effect. I was resigned to my fate, and as the appalling stench overtook me I just hoped that I might die quickly through lack of oxygen. But I soon realized that there was a tiny damaged edge which allowed a minute amount of air into the chamber. I reckoned that if I breathed slowly and carefully I might survive for perhaps twenty hours or so. My only chance of life now, I knew, rested with yourself and Lestrade; but little did I think that the pair of you would be travelling all over the south of England as I lay hopelessly incarcerated, not more than a few hundred yards from your starting point. I did not shout, I knew that no one would hear me. I imagine I must have passed into unconsciousness just a few hours before you found me.'

I agreed, for more than that he would have sunk into a coma from which it would have been impossible to arouse him. I said as much, and Holmes showed how far his recovery had progressed by showing a testy style of speech.

'You had found the clue of the gravestone moss, Watson. Why did you not think to examine its nearest source? Mind you, you did at least notice the stuff, even if you did not realize quite what it was!'

I had to be honest on this point. 'Holmes, it was really Mrs Hudson who recognized it and put us on the right track, even if we did go off in the wrong direction.'

Holmes laughed. 'Huh, fine pair of detectives! It took a simple landlady to put you onto your principal clue. Mind you, she is a very intelligent woman as I have noted many times in the past.'

His eyes glittered with suppressed amusement as he continued, 'She might have made an excellent assistant with my investigations, Watson, had we never met, with the added advantage that she would never have turned herself into my Boswell! Mind you, I could scarcely have sent her to Baskerville Hall or taken her to many of the other places where we have been forced to go together.'

Despite my annoyance at his caustic humour I was forced to chuckle secretly at the thought of a woman of ample proportions, wearing a dustcap and housekeeper's pinafore, brandishing my service revolver.

Sherlock Holmes has always been resilient, and within twenty-four hours nobody could have imagined that he had been through such an horrific near-to-death experience.

As soon as it was clear that he was recovered the King was himself at Holmes's bedside with words of thanks and good cheer. 'Feeling better, Holmes?'

My friend bowed his head as well as he could from his position in the bed. He demonstrated the extent of his recovery with his words.

'Your Majesty, I will be up and about and out of your way on the morrow. I was glad to have been of service to you, but I do apologize for having been instrumental in contributing to the desecration of the remains of one of Your Majesty's past relatives.'

The King glanced left and right with a rather furtive expression on his ample bearded features, then lowered his voice as he said, 'He may have been a relative of mine but he was not one that we spoke of very much. His crypt became rather conveniently overgrown, both literally and in memory! So think nothing of it, Holmes. But I am concerned deeply, not about my so-called relatives of a bygone age, but rather with those of the present time. Young Willy is my cousin, Kaiser of Austro-Hungary and King of Prussia. He has always been arrogant and a thorn in my flesh but I have in the past kept friendly with him for the sake of my late dear mama, who thought quite a lot of him. It was "Willy this and Willy that" all through my childhood and youth, with his being held up before me as an example. But now that dear mama is no longer with us I have scarcely been able to bear his pomposity. I could find only one interest in common with him: we both loved to watch conjurers. By wanting to share with him the pleasure that I got from seeing Goldin perform I unfortunately played into his hands concerning the attempted theft of my Rembrandt. That wretched Frenchwoman had a big hand in it too, but I cannot blame the French for that. The *entente cordiale* is unaffected, but I cannot feel the same towards Germany. This matter has been so serious that I have been on the point of asking my government to consider a declaration of war!'

Holmes surprised us all by getting up from his bed and putting on his dressing gown. He seemed quite recovered now as he stood straight and faced his King.

'Your Majesty, I am just one of your humble subjects,' (I had to stifle a chuckle at Holmes's use of this word to describe himself; anyone less humble than Sherlock Holmes would be difficult to find!) 'but please let me say that I believe that a conflict between Britain and Germany would be a disaster for both sides.'

The King frowned, finding it difficult to fully understand the full meaning of Holmes's words.

He said, 'My dear fellow, surely you have no doubt in your mind that my armies, aye and the great British Navy, would trounce the Germans if it came to war?'

Holmes spoke very quietly as he replied, 'Your forces, excellent as they undoubtedly are, you will agree are thinly spread throughout the world. There would be a terrifying conflict in Europe, and your far-flung forces could not be all brought back for fear of losing the colonies.'

'Ah, but that is where the French come into the picture.

They have a large army well able to take care of Europe!'

Holmes shrugged and played his final card.

'The Germans have already been preparing for such a war in Europe for a long time . . .'

'Nonsense, man!'

'With respect, Your Majesty. I am very much in touch with such things through my brother Mycroft. He has shared with me all the factors and figures and is as worried as I am. There must either be some sort of diplomatic breakthrough, or else Britain must prepare for a conflict to the extent that the Germans are doing.'

Writing this narrative many years later, as I am, it is easy for me to be wise and to see wisdom in Holmes's words. The Great War, as we came to call it, did not occur until a little over a decade later. But it was a terrible conflict which was all but lost by Britain and France, taking a last-minute intervention by the Americans to settle. But King Edward, although an intelligent man, had been brought up to be king on a sea of jingoism. Persons with whom he conversed would never have dared to suggest that the sun could ever set upon the British Empire. Sherlock Holmes was possibly the only man who ever spoke the truth to him upon such subjects.

He was indebted to Holmes and could scarcely do other than forgive him. 'Well, my dear fellow, we must beg to differ upon this subject but we will pursue it further when you are quite recovered.'

He inferred by his deliverance of these words that he was willing to consider that Holmes's recent alarming experience had affected his reasoning powers.

As the King left, with an invitation to dinner if Holmes felt up to it, my friend bowed his head and sighed.

'Alas, Watson, His Majesty is a splendid man, but insulated from the real world!'

The dinner, which Holmes was certainly sufficiently recovered to attend, was a splendid one. There was a delicious turkey main course followed by a steaming currant suet pudding and finally, the *pièce de résistance*, an Ice Bomb. This was dressed with hot chocolate, and the contrast between the hot and cold substances was fascinating to taste.

The King made a very short speech. 'My lords, ladies and gentlemen, this little get together has been hastily arranged as a kind of thanksgiving meal to celebrate the return to us of our dear friend Sherlock Holmes. He is known to you all, not just as a celebrated detective, but as someone to whom you share with me the gratitude for the recovery of that which was lost, be it property, personage or reputation. Please charge your glasses and join me in a toast to Sherlock Holmes!'

As the glasses were raised I glanced around me and for the first time I realized that the King had taken the trouble to invite only those nobles and their ladies who had reason to be grateful to my friend. Lord Derby, whose missing racehorse had been recovered by Holmes; Lady Snowdonia whose diamond tiara glistened, having been restored to her by the great detective; and Sir Charles Faversham whose manuscript had not after all been lost forever, thanks to the sage of Baker Street.

After this short speech by His Majesty there were no other official speeches, save for the odd 'Hear hear' and 'Good old Holmes'.

But the King was known to enjoy some sort of entertainment at his table, and always chose his guests carefully with some kind of expectation in mind. I felt that I had to jump into the fray and told the company the story of the Giant Rat of Sumatra. This created some interest, but I felt that the gathering were a little disappointed in that there seemed to be no indication of an adventure of Sherlock Holmes, told in the first person. The King looked at my friend with a twinkle in his eye.

He spoke kindly. 'Holmes, my dear fellow, you have been through a terrible experience. I feel sure that everyone present will understand how, for the moment, we must rely upon your Boswell to satisfy our curiosity regarding your amazing adventures.'

But Sherlock had been studying the King for some minutes and I could tell from past experience that he was about to make some kind of narration, however minor.

He rose to his feet, so I could only assume that he had something fairly substantial to relate.

'Your Majesty, I will offer you, as my party piece, just an elementary example in the art of deduction concerning the route which you took as you made your way to the dining-room. During my investigations into your missing portrait I had occasion to search every inch of this large house and I discovered that there are no fewer than seven different routes that you could have taken in making your way from your dressing-room to this august apartment. Now I have, I assure you, had no clue given to me as to the actual way you made, but I have been told that you have no favourite path to this room.'

Holmes made a theatrical pause, cutting and lighting a cigar, whilst the King muttered 'Quite true, quite true!' You could otherwise have heard a pin drop with the company on the edges of their seats with the expectation of words of wisdom.

Holmes continued at length. 'Your Majesty left the dressing room, took the longest of the three staircases available and made your way through the small hall. At the end of this you could have taken either the right or left corridor without losing even seconds in time, but the left corridor was the chosen one. You could have walked through any of several doors at this point with equal practicality but you chose the door to the old billiard room and emerged from there into the corridor immediately outside this room.'

There was another silence and everyone looked at the King for comment, which he indeed made.

'Upon my word, you have mapped my route exactly, Holmes, though I fail to see how unless you were told by my servants. I vary my route to the dining-room considerably for reasons which as a detective you will well understand. Am I to take it that your art of deduction allows you to know my movements without any sort of prompting from others?'

I could see that Holmes was enjoying himself now, and was playing his royal fish with skill and style. I had no idea myself as to how he could have known that royal path, and I knew his methods. I awaited his next words with as much curiosity as anyone present.

'How many clocks do you suppose you passed in taking the route you took, Your Majesty?'

The King looked puzzled. He thought carefully before he replied. 'Why, seven, I believe.'

'Just so, and how many would you have encountered on the other routes?'

The King, obviously, had to think most carefully before he replied.

Eventually he said, 'Two on one route, one on another,

none at all on two of them, and two on the others, leaving the route I did take with considerably more than any other. But I quite fail to grasp your point, sir.'

Holmes smiled like a Cheshire cat and added to our bewilderment by saying, 'In this apartment there is a very large clock, with an extremely clear dial, standing exactly opposite to where your Majesty is seated.'

'Why yes, it's the splendid clock presented to my mother by the grateful peasants of Bhaniphur when the British Army finally conquered that province. Really, Holmes, you have me confused.'

Holmes chuckled like a demon king in a pantomime. 'What o'clock do you make it, Sire?'

The King looked at the clock immediately in front of him and said, 'Five past nine of the clock!'

'Is that clock reliable?'

'Why, certainly, but I will check it for you . . .'

The King made a practised move to remove the watch from his vest pocket and discovered that it was not there.

He fumbled a little and then said, 'Bless my soul, I am not wearing my watch, I will dismiss my valet for this! Well, at least, I will remonstrate with him over it.'

I was beginning to see the path that Holmes had taken in his deductions. At last he laid his cards upon the table.

'You see, Your Majesty, I noticed earlier that you had no watch and chain. Now I am observant by nature and have noticed that you have a habit, a quite frequent one, of consulting your Albert. However, I have noticed that if there is a prominently displayed clock in a room you favour casting a glance at it.'

The King nodded. 'Easier than fishing the thing out of

my pocket . . . But what has this to do with the jolly old matter in hand?'

'Whichever route you had chosen would have taken you approximately six minutes to reach the dining-room. By habit, you would have glanced at your watch at least twice during that time, if no clock were in view. But in taking the route that you took you would scarcely have needed to consult your watch with so many clocks in view.'

The King crashed his fist upon the table in appreciation. 'By thunder, you are right, Holmes, and I didn't even notice that I wasn't wearing the wretched thing when I sat at the table because of that huge clock immediately opposite to my seat! Just to think you worked all that out, just from noticing that I was not wearing my watch.'

I did not say so at the time, but I could not help but think that it was one of the most brilliant pieces of deduction that I had ever experienced, even from Sherlock Holmes.

I mused upon who else on earth could have produced such a brilliant piece of reasoning, especially as I'll wager that the whole thing came into Holmes's mind like a flash, with his having to backtrack upon his own thoughts to hit upon its origin. Who else indeed, possibly Mycroft? Yes, Mycroft would have been capable of the deduction itself but would never have been able to produce it because he would have been far too lazy to have done all that leg work which Sherlock had needed in order to have the knowledge to store in his incredible mind.

King Edward sent for his watch, and when the valet brought it to him, I overheard him say, 'Smithers, I at first planned to dismiss you; then I decided that it was a bit drastic, what? Then I was simply going to reprimand you but now I don't believe I will even do that. You see, you have been instrumental in helping to provide me with a really splendid after-dinner story!'

It was true that, from that time on, the King was constantly asked to tell the story of Sherlock Holmes and the Watch.

CHAPTER SIX

The Prize

I was amazed at how quickly Sherlock Holmes had made such a good recovery. Even before we had left Sandringham House he was his old self again. I suppose most people having been imprisoned in a stone sarcophagus in a hidden crypt for several days would have suffered terrible nervous disorders for evermore. But Holmes seemed to be made of stone to rival that used in his incarceration.

When we had been back at Baker Street for a few hours it felt as if we had never left it. There were one or two visitors, people who had heard of Holmes's close call, including Horace Goldin, apologetic for having drawn us into the matter to begin with.

There were some stories in the more sensational newspapers, some of which gave Goldin himself credit for the recovery of the Rembrandt.

He apologized for these. 'This is not what I told these guys, they write whatever they please. I gave them a better story than that. I told them that you had eyes that could see through brick walls, and my manager wants to contact you with a view to a tour of the very finest variety theatres in Britain.'

'Goldin, neither I nor Dr Watson is interested in making theatrical appearances.'

The illusionist played his trump card.

'Not even a tour of American vaudeville houses? Just think, you would be the toast of Broadway.'

Holmes offered Goldin a cigar and said, 'It is out of the question. It is bad enough having Gillette impersonate me on the London stage, though I admit he does it with style. But do you know there are even moving-picture depictions of my exploits, shown on sheets at fairgrounds?'

Goldin appeared a little preoccupied at this point, then took a leather-covered pad from his pocket and scribbled in it with a small pencil, saying, 'You have just given me a flash of inspiration. Suppose the people were to see one of these moving pictures and someone depicted were to step out of the picture and walk around. It would have to be a very well-known figure, someone like yourself, recognized at once both on and off the sheet. Some day, I will use this idea! But to business. My cheque for the amount which I know is correct. This is that amount which you do not vary, save when you omit your fee altogether. I would not allow that, but neither can I quite accept that I should not be allowed to express my most especial thanks. I have a little gift for you.'

I had noticed a bulge under the illusionist's greatcoat, and had wondered why he had made no attempt to divest himself of that garment. So evidently he was secreting there a gift for Holmes. But my friend lifted a hand to halt that movement.

'Mr Goldin, much as I appreciate your kind thought there is no place in my life for a dog, even a Mexican terrier!'

Goldin started, and then withdrew the little animal from beneath his coat, placing it on the floor where it scampered around on its matchsticks of legs and pricked its bat-like ears.

'How did you know that was a live gift?'

'I detected some movement.'

'It could have been a kitten or a monkey.'

'Past observation has told me that a cat would not remain completely silent even under the conditions involved. A monkey would have been unable to make so little movement. It had to be a very small dog.'

I could not resist enquiring, 'But why could it not have been a bulldog pup or a baby spaniel. Admit, Holmes, your naming of the breed was a fortunate guess.'

My friend glared at me as he answered, 'Watson, a puppy is as unable as the other creatures mentioned to remain quite still for so long. It had to be a grown dog, and I know only one species of canine that is small enough when fully grown to fit into Mr Goldin's greatcoat.'

'Ah well, I was growing fond of him already!'

So saying, Horace Goldin picked up the tiny hairless terrier and replaced it inside his coat. Then he picked up his fedora and held it aloft in a farewell salute.

After the illusionist had departed I felt a little uncomfortable for having doubted Holmes's powers. I said as much.

'Think nothing of it, Watson; I am at this present moment delighted with my deliverance from becoming the owner of that wretched little creature. I am not, as you well know, particularly enamoured of dogs; though I am inclined to make an exception of the bloodhound, which is the only useful breed I know.'

It would have been useless to mention breeds which I consider friends of man to someone who does not hunt or shoot and has always seemed to me to have scant regard for those who do.

My friend, still officially convalescent, began an avid search of the day's newspapers. Every so often he would open one of the papers at a certain page and then fold it for reference.

Then, when he had searched all of the papers, he passed them to me in their folded state and said, 'I would like you to study the paragraphs which I have prepared for your attention, Watson . . .'

I glanced swiftly through each piece in turn and noted that they all had one theme in common: they pointed to bones of contention between the British and German governments. They ranged from a report of a skirmish between German and British forces in East Africa where territories adjoined, to various political reports and a speech by the Kaiser which could only be considered as dangerous from an international point of view.

'I'll wager that at least half of these incidents have occurred as a result of the events of the past few days. The politicians will be hard put to calm these situations, but on our side would be well advised to do so, despite the jingoism of our monarch. Oh, by the way, Watson, the King will be paying us a visit shortly.'

I gasped. 'How shortly?'

Holmes glanced at the mantel clock and then studied his hunter as if to verify the accuracy of each.

'If our timepieces are to be relied on, within about five minutes.'

'What? Holmes, do you realize that I cannot possibly

wash, dress and shave in that time, and you are in that old pink dressing robe of yours!'

His reply irritated me greatly. 'You have washed, shaved and dressed once today already, and the King has already seen me at my worst. Admit, Watson, that immediately following a three-day incarceration with a hundred-year-old corpse would not present anyone in the best light. In comparison I am Beau Brummel!'

I had neither time nor opportunity to argue because I could hear the hoofbeats upon the road immediately outside 221B, which told me that the King had indeed arrived. Tremblingly, I crossed to the window and saw that the royal enclosed carriage had drawn up. Fortunately there were no great numbers of people in the street, but I knew that the King would have great difficulty in leaving without a cheering crowd.

As the footman helped the royal bulk from the carriage I noticed that there was another bulky personage still to alight, and when he did so it turned out to be Mycroft!

As I heard the two heavy treads upon the stairs I made a last-minute attempt to tidy the room. But of course it was energy badly spent.

Mrs Hudson entered, cleared her throat and announced, 'Mr Mycroft Holmes and . . . and His Majesty King Edward!'

Holmes arose from his armchair and made what was for him a gesture of sacrifice in brushing the tobacco ash from the front of his dressing gown with his right hand. He bowed his head to the King, as I did, but our recent experience of King Edward's company had shown us that there was no need for us to stand on ceremony.

'Your brother has been telling me how well you have recovered from your ordeal, my dear fellow. I must say you look quite your old self. Well, last time I came here you offered me a cigar out of a coal-scuttle . . . d'ye still keep 'em there?'

I remembered how amused His Majesty had been when offered a corona from that utensil when he had called to consult Holmes regarding the theft of the Crown Jewels. It seemed an age ago, but it had been months rather than years. The King allowed Mycroft to light his cigar with the patent contraption from his pocket. Holmes steered the King to our best armchair and Mycroft to the only other that was in any way respectable.

The King cleared his throat prior to telling us the purpose of his visit. As he spoke, Mycroft looked from one to the other of us with that look of disdain which was part of his expressive repertoire.

But the King was easy in his manner as he spoke. 'I came here in one last attempt to get you to accept a knighthood, Holmes. It has been offered to you before and refused. I, of course, took your point that it might not be seemly for Sir Sherlock Holmes to be scuttling about looking for clues, what? But a little bird has told me that you are considering retirement and whilst this would be a great loss to those threatened by criminal activity it would be well deserved. Of course, you are rather young to be retired. Might I enquire as to the reason for your consideration of it?'

Holmes replied with great sincerity and strength of character as he answered his King. 'Your Majesty, I have followed this profession of mine; one which many may say that I invented for myself; for some five-and-twenty years. My purpose has been to catch the murderer, the thief and the forger, where the police were unable to do so. During a quarter of a century I like to think that I have saved many

lives, and recovered property for both commoners and
kings. But I must not disregard the fact that I have followed my calling for another reason. To excite and exercise my mind and to stretch my intellect to its limits. But
I feel that I have at this point in time reached the peak of
my powers. Inevitably, if I continue into late middle age
my powers of deduction must decline. I do not want that
to happen, so I wish to point my mind and energies in
another direction.'

The King nodded wisely. 'The stock exchange, the diplomatic corps, going to vie with young Mycroft here, what?'

'No, sir, I intend to take myself off to the Sussex coast
and keep bees.'

The King started, seemed about to say something and
appeared to think better of it.

However, he did eventually say, 'Quite so, you must do as
you wish. Well, I have a little gift for you which you must
accept. I insist! Here . . .'

The King crossed to where Holmes was perched upon a
disreputable chair. Sherlock arose and the King took from
his pocket a handsome little leather case. He opened this
and took from it a cravat pin, the like of which I had never
seen before. It was in the form of a miniature hansom cab,
fashioned entirely of diamonds, rubies and other precious
stones laid upon a silver backpiece. It was magnificent and
even Holmes was amazed and delighted with it.

As the King pinned it to Holmes's stock, the detective
said, 'Your Majesty, I cannot tell you how touched and
proud I am to receive this wonderful gift, which although
unexpected gives me such pleasure to receive, especially
from your own hand. I am moreover delighted with the
magnificent taste expressed by my King!'

I believe that Holmes was completely sincere in his words.

The King cleared his throat and said, 'Not at all, my dear chap. I have long noticed that you seem to operate your business largely through the use of hansoms. Alas, they will soon be a memory through these new-fangled motor-cars, but I hope you will always be able to look at this pin and remember the times when the game was afoot . . . a favourite expression of yours, what?'

At this point, the King would have departed and Sherlock Holmes would have admired his pin and it would have been the end of the story. However, there were a couple of twists in its tail which make this one of the most truly unique exploits of my friend Sherlock Holmes that I have ever had the pleasure to narrate.

The King crossed to the window and espied the growing crowd of interested bystanders gathered around the royal carriages.

He grinned wryly to us and said, 'Uneasy lies the head that wears the crown, what? D'ye know I would give anything if there were two of me. Then I could send one of them off in that carriage and have the rest of the day to go quietly off to meet up with my friends, and a certain lady who resides in Belgravia!'

The King jested, but I could see that Holmes had taken him seriously.

'Would Your Majesty be interested in a suggestion as to just how that wish could become reality?'

'Are you serious, Holmes? Have you some sort of flash of inspiration which would grant me a day of freedom?'

'I have indeed, sire. A while ago I discovered to my

irritation that I bore a striking likeness to Sir William Gillette, who took advantage of this by impersonating me in a play. Later, however, I became glad of this likeness when I was able to change places with him in order to evade my enemies.'

The King was amused. 'I take your thought, Holmes, but you and I are of very different build, and you are clean shorn!'

Holmes smiled mysteriously and expounded, 'But Your Majesty and Mycroft are of similar height and build. I have a full grey false beard among my disguise collection and, wearing this, and Your Majesty's hat and cloak, Mycroft could enter your carriage to be driven away. The crowd would soon disperse and I could send Billy to fetch a hansom, in which Your Majesty could travel to Belgravia or wherever else he wished, wearing either Mycroft's ulster or my Inverness cape and deerstalker cap.'

There was a silence that you could have cut with a knife. The King had mischief in his eyes and would be glad to take part in the charade. Mycroft, however, looked at Holmes with abject misery in his face, wanting so to refuse but hardly able to deny his King this service.

The King spoke at last. 'By Jove! You'll do me this small service, will you not, Mycroft?'

Sadly, Mycroft replied, 'If it please Your Majesty.'

And so it was that Mycroft Holmes emerged from 221B Baker Street, wearing the King's cloak and hat, and Sherlock's false beard, to enter the carriage with the cheering crowd quite unaware that they were not rejoicing in seeing their King.

'God save the King!'

'God bless Your Majesty!'

'Good old Teddy!'

All classes of society were present and expressing themselves in their own particular ways.

As the carriage trundled away in the direction of Buckingham Palace the King slapped Holmes upon the back.

'You see, my dear Holmes, I am indebted to you once again.'

Then, as he was helped into Holmes's Inverness and deerstalker, he added, 'You know, there must be some little thing that I can do for you, Holmes, you are such a splendid chap. After all, what's the good of being a king if you can't have jam for tea?'

Suddenly, as Mrs Hudson aided with the tidying of her monarch, an all but crafty expression crossed Holmes's face.

He hesitated a little as he spoke. 'Well, sire, your kindness to me has been phenomenal already. But . . . well, there is one little thing which occurs to me.'

'Some honour or order, just name it and it is yours, man!'

'Your Majesty, I have resided for quite a long time at these rooms, which are shared with me by my friend and colleague, Dr Watson. Of course these rooms are modest but extremely comfortable and are owned by our splendid landlady Mrs Hudson.'

The King touched Holmes's deerstalker in salute to the good lady who bobbed a quick curtsy.

He said, 'Quite so I have noticed how well you are taken care of here; I am sure that Mrs Hudson is a gem!'

'But sire, the good lady is about to lose this property to some sort of rebuilding scheme, and although she will be compensated it will not really recompense her for the loss of this splendid house.'

King Edward was trying to retain his interest out of politeness, but I could see that he was beginning to verge on impatience whilst retaining his splendid manners.

He said, 'Quite so, business may be the heart of our nation, Holmes, but sometimes one wonders quite how far these speculative johnnies should be allowed to go. Of course, if the Crown had any connection in the matter you could have relied upon my intervention.'

At this point I shot a quick glance at Mrs Hudson; she was and remains a highly intelligent woman and I read the joy in her face, subdued as it was. I imagined that she was thinking, 'Mr Holmes, you've done it!'

Holmes at this point dropped his bombshell and said, 'As it happens the Crown is indeed involved. Mrs Hudson, please run and fetch that letter of yours to show to His Majesty.'

The good lady fairly dashed from the room, and whilst she was gone Holmes explained to the King the details concerning the impending demolition of 221B Baker Street.

His Majesty nodded with comprehension. 'Ah, now this I can help you with and it would be churlish of me to refuse to.'

Then, as Mrs Hudson returned and showed him the letter, he said to her, 'Dear lady, fear not, your home is safe from my people, and you have my promise on that!'

So it was that Mrs Hudson was able to retain her excellent establishment, not just for the remainder of Sherlock Holmes's residence there, but for a number of years thereafter. Then when eventually she, like Holmes, decided to retire she was able to sell 221B and purchase a cottage upon the South Coast. She tended her roses at Lancing whilst Holmes tended his bees at Fowlhaven.

As for Horace Goldin, I need hardly tell the reader of his adventures since those days. He continues at this time of writing as the Royal Illusionist, and seems to produce a new and highly topical mystery all but weekly. He has his imitators, of course, but he remains to me 'The Rembrandt of Mystery'!